D1536490

BERNADETTE
Our Lady's Little Servant

BERNADETTE

Our Lady's Little Servant

Written by Hertha Pauli

Illustrated by Georges Vaux

IGNATIUS PRESS   SAN FRANCISCO

Published by Farrar, Straus & Cudahy, Inc.
A Vision Book
Reprinted with permission of the Estate of Hertha Pauli

.

Cover art by Christopher J. Pelicano
Cover design by Riz Boncan Marsella

Published by Ignatius Press, San Francisco, 1999
ISBN 978-0-89870-760-1
Library of Congress catalogue number 99-72129
Printed by Thomson-Shore, Dexter, MI (USA); RMA574LS654, June, 2011

". . . and the last shall be first"
(Mt 19:30)

CONTENTS

I

WOOD-GATHERING

IT HAPPENED ON A THURSDAY. Dates were hard to remember for little Bernadette, but she always kept the days of the week in mind. After that eleventh of February 1858 she would always love Thursdays.

The day started badly. The weather was foggy and cold. From the snow-covered peaks of the Pyrenees the clouds rolled down the valley, hanging low over the roofs and steeples of the small French town of Lourdes. "You stay home today", said Mother. Bernadette's cough had grown worse lately; she had been out in the rain too much, picking up rags and old iron, for which the scrap dealer might give her a few coppers. In the Soubirous household a few coppers meant a great deal.

Father was out looking for work. It was hard to find nowadays. Now and then he made a whole franc at a time at the hospice, the school and hospital run by the Sisters of Nevers. Father's job there was to collect the dirty dressings and carry them to the rubbish dump. Brother Jean, the seven-year-old, had sneaked out into the alley.

Longingly Bernadette looked out of the window. She knew what made her cough and gasp for breath all the time: it was her asthma. Perhaps it was what kept her from growing. She had turned fourteen on the seventh of January; her sister Toinette was not even twelve, but already she was bigger and stronger than Bernadette, who seemed unable to catch up with her. At times it hurt a little to hear everyone say that you did not look your age.

There was no glass in the window Bernadette was looking out of. It really was just a hole in the wall, with some rusty iron bars across. All she could see through it was the manure pile in the little stone yard. But she could always imagine the towering walls of the old fortress, the Citadel, in the rear and the crooked alley in front, where the other girls were now probably skipping rope on the cobblestones. Bernadette loved the game. She could not skip as well as the others, but she was glad to hold the rope for them.

Her sister Toinette tried hard to quiet the youngest, who was going on three but was so small he was still called "the baby". He was hungry and whimpered. Mother had rolled up the children's straw mattress and was just making Father's and her bed. Suddenly the door opened, and Jean was flung in by a broad-shouldered figure.

It was Uncle André. He said, "*Bonjour*—good day", but the look on his face was not a good sign. Mother constantly feared that her cousin might throw the family out on the street. He owned the house. He lived upstairs, had his stone-cutter's shop in front, and for more than a year now he had let the Soubirous live in the back room behind the barred window, for the love of God. The room had a cracked stone floor and damp stone walls; you could get in only by a narrow, unlit passageway, and it had given the whole house its name: the Old Jail. For it had indeed been the town jail until it was no longer thought fit even for criminals.

"Better keep an eye on the rascal, Louise", the uncle growled at Mother. "Found him begging at Estrade's back door."

Mother raised the stick that was still in her hand from stretching the blankets, but then she shook her head. "You must be mistaken, André. Our children don't beg. We're not starving."

Her cousin glanced at the burned-out fireplace. "Ask him", he said dryly and sat down on the one wobbly chair.

"I've done nothing wrong", Jean pleaded. "She told me to come to the back door."

"She? Mademoiselle Estrade? The tax collector's sister? But how do you know her?"

Jean gulped. "She doesn't know me", he said quickly. "I never told her my name."

"She told me everything", said the uncle. "It began when he disturbed her prayers in church. Seems he used to scratch the wax drippings off the candlesticks and eat them. She's been feeding him ever since."

An embarrassed silence followed.

The uncle went on. "Of course, I didn't tell his name, either, Louise. I don't want to hear about you from Estrades now. They're high class."

There were tears in Mother's eyes.

I'm never hungry in church, Bernadette thought. She said, "Thank you, Uncle", as he left. He isn't going to throw us out, she thought.

Mother dabbed at her eyes and said, "We'll have soup today." The children pricked up their ears. Soup—when? Now, or not till Father got home, whenever that would be?

Bernadette went to the hearth to poke in the embers. "Mother," she said, "there's no more wood."

"I'll get some, Mother; can I get some?" Toinette was on her feet. Gathering driftwood and fallen branches on public land was a favorite chore of poor children.

"All right", Mother nodded. But when Bernadette asked permission to go along, she shook her head vigorously. "The doctor said you mustn't get wet and cold."

Steps clattered in the hallway, and a girl even bigger than Toinette burst in. She gave a breezy "*Bonjour, Louise*" to Mother and a slap on the back to Bernadette. She hugged Toinette, who cried, "Jeanne!" and started chattering.

Jeanne lived next door and was about Bernadette's age, but her friend was Toinette. The girls' mothers used to go out to work together. Jeanne had started coming to the Old Jail last fall, when Toinette had been alone and Bernadette at a nearby village, helping on a farm. It was an odd thing, Bernadette thought; her happiest moments on the farm had come with the sheep; her worst, when the farmer's wife tried to teach her the catechism and shouted, "You fool, you'll never learn a thing!" She was glad to be back home and going to school at the hospice. Not, of course, to the regular convent school, but to the weekly catechism class that the chaplain of the hospice taught to the children of the poor, to prepare them for their

First Communion. She only hoped to keep up with it, although she could neither read nor write and spoke only a patois, a local dialect spoken in Lourdes, not the French of the catechism. It was such a disgrace to be fourteen and not to have made your First Communion!

Toinette was hunting for her *sabots*. "Where are you going?" Jeanne asked.

"To pick up wood."

"Wait", Bernadette said and brought the basket they always carried for rags. Toinette had found the wooden shoes and was putting them on. Bernadette already wore hers, and stockings too, against the chill of the stone floor. She could never go barefoot at home, like other children.

"I'll go, too", Jeanne declared. "It's fun; let's all go together."

Bernadette looked at Mother. She knew Mother did not like to say no to a neighbor. "On the farm," she said, "I went out in all kinds of weather."

"Well," Mother sighed, "all right. But take your cape, at least."

Bernadette picked up the old black cloak, wrapped it about her shoulders, and tied the striped wool kerchief on the side of her head. Then she ran after the others.

They took turns carrying the basket down the alley and across the country road that ran along the edge of town, past the Citadel, to the old stone bridge across the river. The mountains were invisible. The clouds hung low in the valleys, hiding the wooded slopes. They walked around the back of the cemetery, and on a hillside known as Field of Paradise they found some rags but hardly any wood.

Under the bridge the children met an old woman in a white bonnet. She was doing somebody's laundry in the swift, glacier-fed river. "What are you doing here in this frightful cold?" she asked, her few teeth chattering.

"We're after wood."

"Go to Sawmill Meadow. They've been cutting trees. You'll find all you want there."

They strolled across the bridge. "Come on", Jeanne said. "I know the way."

Bernadette was worried. Picking up things on the common land of the town and along the river banks was all right, but the meadow belonged to the sawmill, and the wood on it was better left alone. Only last year Father had been in terrible trouble over a plank that someone had left by the roadside. He brought it home—the Old Jail had been wonderfully warm that day, she remembered—and then the police came. Father went with them and did not come home for two weeks, and now Bernadette sometimes heard people mutter, "Once a thief, always a thief."

"They'll say we stole", she warned.

"Coward", sneered Jeanne.

But then they were across the bridge and heading

for the sawmill. Beyond the mill-stream to their right, in the great, elbow-shaped bend of the river, Sawmill Meadow was strewn with enough timber to warm the whole town. The mill, that day, was deserted. There was a wooden bridge, and Jeanne and Toinette, who had been walking ahead, stopped on it to have a look at the canal.

"Let's follow it and see where it goes", Bernadette said when she caught up with them. There was no one in sight anywhere, but she was still afraid of being on someone else's property.

Toinette ignored her and followed Jeanne across the bridge into the meadow. They did not go where the cut trees lay, however, but to the river bank and downstream, to a grove that was as thick as a small forest. There they found some dry branches and dragged them along under their arms. Bernadette came slowly after them. Behind the grove was nothing but a narrow point of rocks and sand between the river and the mill-stream. Straight ahead, across the canal, rose the rock of Massabieille, a wild and lonely place about which all sorts of evil tales were told. Shepherds crossed themselves as they hurriedly drove their flocks past, and the only man said to be unafraid of the spot was the swineherd who called for the pigs of Lourdes in the morning and returned them at night, after a day of rooting around Massabieille.

Bernadette paused for breath, gazing at the rock across the shallow water. It looked like a tremendous sponge of granite, moss-covered and honeycombed with caves. Directly in front of her was a grotto, a small cave with an arched entrance ringed with briars and an oval niche, like a window, above and slightly to one side. A wild rosebush, thorny and bare now, climbed up the rock to the niche.

"Look", Jeanne cried, pointing to some old driftwood near the mouth of the cave. Then Toinette spotted some branches that had been carried down by the mill-stream and washed ashore. They took off their *sabots*, and Jeanne flung hers over the canal. Toinette kept her pair in her hand as the two of them waded across, lugging their bundles. The water was knee-deep and so cold that Toinette could not hold back a few squeals, but Jeanne only gritted her teeth and snorted with disdain when Bernadette called after them to pull their skirts down.

Ashore, the two dropped their loads and started rubbing their feet warm with their petticoats. Bernadette threw rocks into the water to make stepping-stones so she could cross without wetting her feet. They simply dropped out of sight. "Throw in a few from your side", she called.

"I'll come back and carry you over", Toinette offered.

Bernadette shook her head. "You're too small. Jeanne, you carry me. You're strong."

Jeanne swore. Bernadette told her not to. Jeanne laughed and shrugged her shoulders. "If you want to cross, cross. If not, stay where you are." And off she went with Toinette, following the canal to the point where it met the river.

Bernadette went to look for a shallower place but could find none. Reluctantly she decided to cross as the others had. When she bent down to take off her *sabots*, she heard a noise as of a sudden gust of wind. She turned around, but no tree in the meadow was stirring.

She stooped again to pull off a stocking and heard the same rustle. Frightened, she stood up and looked at the grotto. She was afraid—but not afraid as she had been at other times, wanting to run away. It never occurred to her to run away.

The oval niche above the rosebush seemed suddenly aglow. The bush trembled a little. Two small golden roses appeared to flower on it. Bernadette stared in wonder. She saw the roses had not grown on the bush that bent beneath them: they adorned two small bare feet under the hem of a shimmering white gown. The gown enveloped the loveliest little figure, no larger than Bernadette herself, standing at the opening above the bush. It was a girl—a little young Lady of sixteen or seventeen—smiling.

Bernadette could say nothing, think nothing. She rubbed her eyes and opened them again. The little Lady was still there. On her head was a white veil that fell on her back and all but covered her hair. She wore a blue sash. Her eyes were blue.

Bernadette fell on her knees. Her trembling fingers groped in her pocket and found her rosary. She tried to cross herself but could not bring her hand up to her forehead as usual. It fell back limply.

The lovely figure turned aside for an instant. Bernadette clutched her rosary. Then the young Lady in white looked back at her with a smile—and now she, too, held a rosary. The beads were not dark and plain like Bernadette's, though, but shimmering white like the little Lady's gown, and the golden chain shone like the roses on her feet.

With infinite grace the Lady made the Sign of the Cross. Bernadette's numb hand followed, and again the Lady smiled. Bernadette said an Our Father and began the Hail Marys. The Lady likewise passed her beads through her fingers but did not move her lips. The rosary gleamed in her hands. It reached to her knees, and the shining cross on it hung from a locket shaped like a heart.

When Jeanne and Toinette came back from their stroll down the river bank, Bernadette seemed not to see them. She was on her knees, still staring at the niche above the grotto. "Save your prayers for Sunday", Jeanne called across the canal.

Bernadette did not answer. Toinette called her by name, but she did not turn her head. "That's all she's good for", Jeanne said contemptuously. "Praying."

Bernadette looked at them and got up slowly, as

though waking from a dream. "What are you doing there?" Toinette asked.

Bernadette said nothing.

Her sister was disgusted. "You should have stayed at home, or you should have been picking up wood."

Bernadette let the rosary slide back into her pocket. "Didn't you see anything?"

"No", they both said. "Was there anything?"

A strange smile flitted over Bernadette's pale face, and her large, dark, deep-set eyes seemed far away.

"What was it? What was it?" cried the two on the other side of the mill-stream, dancing with curiosity.

Bernadette said nothing. She looked at them, calmly now, and bent down to pull off her second stocking.

"What did you see? Tell us!"

Bernadette was barefoot. She picked up her stockings and *sabots* and started for the water. "I saw a Lady in white," she said, "with a blue sash and a yellow rose on each foot."

Jeanne burst out laughing. "You just tell that to the others, and you'll be the joke of the town!"

"Then let's not tell anyone", Bernadette said thoughtfully, wading.

Jeanne and Toinette stood with open mouths, gaping at the way she crossed the stream.

"Heavens," she laughed as she came out, "what was the matter with you? It feels warm."

2

ROCKSLIDE

JEANNE went home alone.

For a short while she had waited for the Soubirous girls, munching a crust of bread that she had found in her pocket. Toinette was snapping at her sister, who sat on a rock, putting on her stockings. She did not seem to feel the cold. Pretty soon Jeanne got up, lifted her bundle of wood on her head, and left.

A steep path ran up behind the grotto. She followed it to the forest road, wondering what was the matter with Bernadette. The water had been icy. Jeanne had been unable to get her feet back into her *sabots*. How could Bernadette suddenly stand it better? No sickly runt was going to show up Jeanne.

How could she see a girl Jeanne could not see? All the way back to town Jeanne was balancing wood on her head and turning over riddles inside it.

In front of her house she met her friend Pauline. Jeanne threw her bundle against the door, and the two girls went down the street together. "Were you out alone?" Pauline asked.

"I took the two Soubirous along", said Jeanne. "We were at Massabieille."

Her friend shuddered. "Weren't you scared? They say that place is the Devil's."

"I'm scared of nothing", said Jeanne.

She wondered whether to bring up Bernadette's story. Pauline's folks were not rich, but they were not as poor as the Soubirous or Jeanne's mother. They owned a plaster statue of the Virgin that was used each year in the Corpus Christi procession. That gave them a certain authority in such matters.

"Bernadette told us she saw something", Jeanne said. "But we're not supposed to talk about it."

Pauline laughed at the idea of Jeanne taking orders from Bernadette. "What did she see?"

"A girl in white."

Pauline hastened to cross herself.

The water! It flashed through Jeanne's mind. Could the Devil not warm up a stream? Aloud she said, "I guess she's fibbing. I don't think she saw a thing. Let's take her out again with some of the girls and see what happens."

Somewhat hesitantly, Pauline agreed.

The sun, just before setting, had pierced the clouds and gilded the battlements of the Citadel, but the alley at the foot of the massive walls already lay in dusk. The Old Jail was now warmed by a blazing fire. Toinette had been eating some corn mush while Bernadette sat silently by the window that was really just a barred hole in a prison wall. All this time she had hardly spoken, had hardly eaten, had only smiled to herself.

Father was in bed with his face to the wall. The baby was asleep. Mother spread the children's mattress on the floor and told little Jean to say his prayers and go to sleep. He obeyed at once. It was quiet in the Old Jail. The fire crackled softly, and the tale of the white Lady burned on Toinette's lips.

"I'm going to comb your hair", Mother told the two girls.

Toinette ran to the window to undo her braids. Bernadette went out into the dark passageway, where they had thrown the wood that was not dry enough to burn. Toinette tried bravely to gulp the secret down as Mother bent over her, but it stuck in her throat and made her cough once or twice. "What's wrong?" Mother asked. "Are you sick, too?" Toinette shook her head. "Hold still", said Mother.

In the passage, Bernadette was noisily stripping branches. She can't hear us now, Toinette thought and whispered close to her mother's ear: "There's nothing wrong with me, but Bernadette—" She broke off.

The comb jerked impatiently. "What about Bernadette? Speak up!"

Toinette tried to give a faithful account. When she had finished, Louise Soubirous wrung her hands. "Am I not wretched enough? Must everything happen to me?" She called Bernadette and got the story from her. She became angrier and angrier. She grabbed the blanket-stretcher and lashed out at Bernadette, then at Toinette.

"You've made Mother hit me", Toinette shrieked.

Bernadette did not answer.

Louise Soubirous seized her daughter's arms and shook her. "Your eyes must have played you a trick", she cried. "You must have seen a white stone—"

"No, she had a lovely face", Bernadette said quietly.

Her mother let go. "We must pray", she said, suddenly frightened. "It may be the soul of one of our relatives in purgatory—"

"Are you all possessed by the Devil?" Father shouted from his bed. "Stop that nonsense! I want to sleep."

Only Bernadette could not sleep.

In the morning Aunt Bernarde came to call. Bernadette was her godchild and fond of her, but she thanked heaven that Father was out, so there would be no talk about money. Aunt Bernarde had loaned Father money years ago, after he lost the mill where

Bernadette was born. But today she had no chance to mention it, anyway. She no sooner came in than Mother tearfully consulted her about Bernadette's strange experience.

Even the aunt was a little alarmed.

"Marie Bernarde"—as godmother she liked to address Bernadette by her full Christian name—"you must be careful. The Devil sometimes disguises himself, to deceive people. You think you're looking at a pretty girl, and before you know it you're face to face with the Devil."

Bernadette shook her head. "The Devil can't be so beautiful", she said with conviction. And when her godmother seemed unimpressed, she added, "He wouldn't hold a rosary, either."

This carried weight with Aunt Bernarde. She was about to change the subject when a whole crowd of girls swept in: Jeanne, Pauline, and some others. They wanted to take Bernadette along, to get more wood and have another look at the grotto—

Had Jeanne been tattling? There was no time to ask.

Mother drew herself up and cut them short: "Bernadette is not going back there. You leave us alone."

They withdrew in a hurry.

"That's final", Louise gruffly told her daughter.

The godmother saw tears welling up in Bernadette's eyes. "Go to confession, Marie Bernarde", was her consoling advice.

That day, and most of the next, Bernadette was kept at home. She would not talk to anyone about what she had seen. Toinette teased her: "Maybe you think the white Lady is waiting?"

Bernadette shook her head. "I am waiting."

Late on Saturday she went to confession. She began with an old sin that still bothered her. It was a sin of injustice, committed when she was minding the sheep on the farm. She had preferred one lamb above the rest, feeding it bread and salt.

"But why did you prefer that one lamb to all the others?" asked the voice from the confessional.

"Because it was the smallest," she replied, "and I like all small things."

She heard that this was no sin, so she dared to tell of her encounter with the young Lady who also was so small—no taller than Bernadette herself—but so beautiful. Curiously, it did not seem to surprise the priest.

"Would it be a sin if I went to the grotto again, Father?"

"No, my child", said the voice from the confessional. "Just say your beads diligently, trust in God, and be on time for ten o'clock Mass tomorrow."

The girls of Lourdes went to Mass in their bright Sunday finery, but Bernadette always wore the same dark, shabby dress under her cloak. After the service it looked as though a swarm of butterflies were fluttering about the church steps.

A girl named Catherine spoke up first: "We'll go with you, Bernadette, if you want to go again—won't we, girls?" She was the prettiest and could hardly wait to compare herself with the inhabitant of the grotto.

"Yes—yes—we'll go if you'll go again—"

"I'd like to," Bernadette said, "but I don't dare ask my mother."

"Let's all ask her!"

At the Old Jail the adventure seemed doomed to fail. Bernadette said little, and Mother was firm. The most that Toinette finally could wheedle out of her was a sour, "Go and ask your father." Her tone suggested that she knew what he would say.

They found him at the postmaster's house, cleaning the stable. This time Bernadette asked, but Father merely said, "No!" in a voice that carried a mile.

The postmaster heard it in the house and came out to ask what was going on. "Let the little one go, François", he said when he had heard the story. "If what she sees is holding a rosary, it can't be evil."

François Soubirous looked helplessly from the postmaster to the flock of girls. Should he please his wife or the man who had given him a day's work? "All right," he said, "go. But only for a quarter of an hour."

"That's not enough, Father", Bernadette said.

"All right—go!" He almost sobbed.

Out they ran in triumph. But some began to feel a

bit uneasy now that their idea was being taken seriously. After all, everyone knew the stories about Massabieille. A little one named Marie suggested taking some holy water along, to make whatever appeared out there go away if it was the Devil's. They went back to the Old Jail, but Louise Soubirous had just stepped out to see a neighbor. There was no time to wait, so Toinette took a bottle from the mantel, and they trotted back to church in a body, filled the bottle from the holy water fount, and started on their way.

They were still in their Sunday best—still a butterfly swarm—but the tiny one in the dark cloak was now in the front row with Toinette and Marie, who had the holy water bottle in her pocket. On their heels came Pauline; she had promised Jeanne to keep an eye on Bernadette while Jeanne rounded up some more friends and went ahead to the grotto. It was all Pauline could do to keep Bernadette in sight. Bernadette turned off the forest road and headed for the big rock. The little one who used to gasp after a minute's play was all but flying through the underbrush, over the boulder-strewn ground, ahead of everyone else.

A man stood on the hilltop. "Don't go down there," he called to the flock of girls, "or the Blessed Virgin will catch you!"

Bernadette plunged down the steep path. Quaking in her *sabots*, Pauline followed. At the bottom she turned and looked for Jeanne. But Jeanne was nowhere.

Bernadette was kneeling. The others knelt down, too, and began to say their rosaries. Pauline saw the pale face of Catherine, the pretty one, and the serious face of little Marie. Pauline sank to her knees.

"It's getting brighter", Bernadette whispered.

"Where? Where?" gasped excited voices.

Pauline could see nothing. She looked at the grotto and at the niche and saw no brightness. She looked higher and was terrified to see Jeanne's angry, twisted face on the cliff.

Pauline shook like a leaf at the sight. Jeanne's possessed, she thought; it's she who is the Devil's!

Jeanne quivered with rage. The runt had beaten her again! She held on to a bush and leaned far over the edge. Bernadette, on her knees below, was staring upward, at a point below Jeanne. Her face looked strange. The girls behind her were excitedly mumbling their rosaries. Jeanne saw Pauline, her eyes wide with fear.

"They didn't wait for us", Jeanne hissed at her companions. "Watch me give them a scare!"

Below, Bernadette had put her arm around Catherine and was pointing at the rock. Marie got the holy water bottle from her pocket and thrust it into Bernadette's hand.

Jeanne shouted: "Ask if she comes from God or the Devil!"

With a choked cry, Pauline leaped up below and ran off in panic.

Bernadette threw the holy water. Her lips barely moved. Her face lit up in a smile.

She didn't ask, Jeanne thought; she must have been afraid to ask. . . . She jerked back. The stone under her hand was coming loose. It was the size of a large loaf of bread, too heavy to lift. "Wait, I'll take care of your white girl!" she cried, rolling the stone over the edge.

The stone fell, hit the rock Bernadette was kneeling on, and bounced off. It threaded a path through the group of kneeling girls and fell into the millstream.

Jeanne heard cries of terror, Toinette screeching above the rest: "She's dead—Bernadette is dead—" Jeanne stumbled to her feet and ran blindly down the path. Toinette clutched Bernadette's shoulders. Bernadette did not move.

A few girls ran up the path for help. Toinette let go of her sister, stared about her, and tore after them, sobbing wildly. "Help," her voice rang down, "help— Mother—Mother—" It grew fainter and faded away.

Still, Bernadette did not move. Her face was white, her eyes wide open. She's dead, Jeanne thought and stared at the kneeling figure; I've killed her. The holy water bottle lay on the ground, broken. The girls who remained were in tears. Jeanne did not see who they were. One of them jumped up, crying, "You've killed her; I'm going back to tell Louise!" Jeanne did not protest.

She tried to raise Bernadette to her feet, but all the strength she was so proud of seemed to have drained away from her. She could not move that rigid body any more than she could have moved the rock of Massabieille.

Fear gripped Jeanne. She drew back and wanted to flee, but her legs buckled. Suddenly she screamed—a piercing, agonized cry that echoed from the rock and shrilled over the river and up the mountainside. She screamed until two horrified women came down the rocky path, wailing, "Holy Mother of God, it's the little Soubirous girl!"

Bernadette did not move.

The women tried to lift her, but the slight body seemed too heavy for them, too. They ran to the nearby mill and called the miller, who was their son and nephew. For a while he just stood gazing at Bernadette as though afraid to touch her. Bernadette knelt as before, still and white as wax. Tears streamed from the wide-open eyes that were fixed on the niche, and she was smiling. The miller looked up. "She's beautiful!"

She's alive! it came to Jeanne in a flash.

"We must take her home with us", said the miller's mother.

He took Bernadette's right arm; he looked like a man straining to unbend the arm of a statue. Her eyes remained on the niche. She never murmured, only breathed faster after struggling. He wiped her eyes, put his hand over them, and tried to make her bend her head. She raised it again, reopened her eyes, and went on smiling.

The miller and his mother dragged Bernadette by the hands up the path. His aunt and the girls pushed from behind; Jeanne followed. Bernadette kept trying to go down again, still without saying a word, and with her wide-open eyes fixed on something above them. The husky miller was dripping sweat when they got to the top.

They dragged her through the woods to the mill. From time to time the miller wiped off her tears. It was not until they were actually on the threshold of the mill that she lowered her head and the color returned to her cheeks.

She was led into the kitchen and made to sit down. Jeanne crouched in a corner. "What do you see in that hole there?" the miller asked Bernadette. "You must see something dreadful."

"Oh, no", she said. "I see the loveliest Lady; she has a rosary on her arm, and her hands are joined." She pressed her palms together.

More and more people came. Soon the mill was crowded. Someone muttered, "There's Louise." Jeanne tightened up.

"My God, I had forbidden her to go!" Louise Soubirous burst in, screaming. She had a stick in her hand: "I'll teach you to make everyone run after you—"

Jeanne ran out of her corner. "I did it! Hit me! It was my fault!"

No one paid any attention to her. It was as if she had not been in the room. The women tried to soothe Louise, who broke down in front of her daughter, sobbing, "What will they say of us—nothing but shame and disgrace all the time, and now this—"

Jeanne stood before Bernadette. Bernadette sat on a kitchen stool, smiling through the tears that ran down her face, and did not seem to know what went on around her. "I might have killed a saint", Jeanne whispered.

Bernadette smiled through the tears that ran down her face.

3

PROMISES

AUNT BERNARDE kept the inn in town. It was always busy, but never more than on Sundays. Then half the men in Lourdes would drop in for a glass of wine or two. They never changed their tables or the hours when they came and left; one could tell time at the inn by their arrival. When the miller showed up two hours late that Sunday, the hostess personally took his wine to the table he shared with three other millers. She demanded to know what had kept him.

The miller told her. He told the whole story—as much as he knew of it—and before he was through everyone around was listening.

Aunt Bernarde threw up her hands. "My God, that child! What can she be thinking of, to go down there!"

A fat woman in a widow's dress, who sat alone at the next table, made the Sign of the Cross.

Aunt Bernarde looked anxiously about her. She would have liked to run to her godchild, but with the inn filling up by the minute, that was impossible. Even women came in now, chattering about the state in which the children had come back from Massabieille. One of them was the baker's wife, who lived next door to the Old Jail. "Did you hear what happened to Bernadette?" asked the worried godmother.

"Hear it, my dear? I saw it", said the baker's wife. "Your poor sister was visiting me when it happened. I went out to the mill with her. We just brought the little one back. She came along like a lamb, but the other mothers had a time getting their children home."

The black satin of the widow's dress rustled as she bent forward curiously. "Do you think she made it all up?"

The baker's wife ignored her. She turned a group of women: "Let's look at this grotto and find

out what these children see there!" A moment later
they were gone.

The place was getting so crowded that half the
guests had to stand. Only the chairs at the widow's
table stayed empty. "What do I owe?" she finally
asked in a loud voice, jingling the change in her
purse.

"One moment, Madame", said the hostess. She ran
to greet a lively, gray-haired woman who stood un-
certainly in the door of the inn. It was seldom hon-
ored by the teacher at the public high school. "Good
afternoon, Mademoiselle", gushed Aunt Bernarde.
"Won't you sit down?"

"Thank you, no. I just want to ask about those
children. I saw a few carrying on as if they'd seen a
ghost. What happened?"

Bernarde told her.

"Visions at Massabieille?" The schoolmistress was
shocked. "Why, they take the pigs there!"

"That place is haunted", the widow said gloomily,
getting up with an effort.

The schoolmistress swept her skirts aside as though
afraid to soil them. Then she said good-bye cordially
to Aunt Bernarde, who saw her to the door.

The woman in black was left standing by herself.
Despite her weight, one could see that she had once
been pretty. Most everyone in Lourdes remembered
her as a servant, and not a well-recommended one, at
that. Her master had married her and then died. The

money he left her had improved her station in life but not her reputation. Memories are long in small French towns. The widow offered the biggest candles in church and bought only the best of everything now, and yet nobody liked her. She spent hours at the inn, surrounded by gossip, but nobody gossiped with her. All she could do to pass the time was eat and grow fatter and fatter.

She made another quick Sign of the Cross and sighed. She felt sorry for herself until she remembered the new dress she was getting, of the finest Belgian lace. The thought cheered her up. Anyway, people were just as nasty to others—to the Soubirous, for instance. They had to live in the Old Jail, after years of being kicked from place to place, and for company they had to look to the haunts of Massabieille.

The widow threw some coins on the table and made her way to the door. The baker's wife and her friends were just coming back from the grotto. "What did you see?" asked the widow.

They shrugged and pushed past her. But when Aunt Bernarde came and asked, the baker's wife said, "All we saw was a hole in the rock and a dead rosebush."

The widow, still on the threshold, looked back almost with glee before she turned and waddled down the street.

The women nudged each other, looking after her.

"Superstitious fool", muttered the baker's wife. Then they went to meet their husbands.

The next day, when the inn was closed for cleaning, Aunt Bernarde wrapped up some food that the Sunday guests had left and went to see her godchild. It was high noon, but she always needed a moment or two to get used again to the twilight in the Old Jail. She laid the package on the stone sill. Toinette and Jean edged toward it until their mother snatched it away.

"Don't touch that!" she scolded. "Bernadette must have food, said the doctor. You think I don't know that you two always eat your share and hers, too? But not this time, you hear?"

The two children stood quietly by the barred window, their eyes on the food.

A whimper came from the darkest corner of the room. Aunt Bernarde looked and saw Bernadette there, with the baby in her lap. The godmother went to her. "Don't you want to eat, Marie Bernarde?"

Bernadette shook her head. She sat with her eyes on the baby, gently rocking him. The whimpers ceased.

Mother said she would divide the food later. The child was all right now; she just had not let her go out yet.

"Not even to catechism class?" asked the godmother. Mother shook her head. "She was coughing so—"

Aunt Bernarde swallowed the speech she had prepared for her godchild. She wished the poor thing would not huddle in the corner like this, frozen in misery. If one could only do something to help!

"One thing I know", Mother sighed. "I won't let her go there again."

"You're so right", agreed the godmother.

Bernadette turned up her face; it was bathed in tears. "The Lady will forget me", she said in a dead voice.

On Tuesday the widow had a last fitting for her new lace dress. The seamstress, a sour-faced young woman, proudly draped the masterpiece over the back of a chair, but her customer hardly glanced at it. She was lost in thought. "Have you heard the stories about Massabieille?" she asked at last.

"I should say so", the seamstress said matter-of-factly, smoothing the dress on the chair. "A white dress with a blue sash."

This confused the widow, for the dress on the chair was black with a white sash. "It fits", the other said, lifting up the black dress.

"What on earth are you talking about?" the widow asked and began to take off her gown.

The seamstress hesitated. "At first, of course, I didn't believe a word of it. You naturally expect lies from the child of a thief—"

"They're so poor", said the widow. She stood in her petticoats now, bulging all over and ready to be fitted. "They get no rest, poor souls", she said compassionately.

"That's it", said the seamstress. "It was the dress that made me think of it. Last night I kept seeing it before me—white dress, blue sash, a rosary—and then it came to me in a flash: I made that dress myself for poor Mademoiselle Elise, the chairlady of our Children of Mary Society. . ." She broke off and pulled the new black dress over her customer's head.

The widow made gurgling sounds under the mass of lace. "But," she gasped when she could see again, "but the chairlady died last year!"

"Yes", said the seamstress through the teeth in which she held her pins. She started buttoning up the dress. "I've always had a special devotion to the souls in purgatory."

The widow panted. She had put on weight since the last fitting; the dress simply would not close. Pop! went a button, but she was too excited to notice. "The chairlady of the Children of Mary in purgatory!" she whispered, and her eyes were full of fear.

"She must be the Lady in the grotto", the seamstress said and gave up trying to close the buttons. Her thin hands dropped. For a moment she stood absentmindedly repeating, "White dress, blue sash . . . Oh, excuse me, Madame!" She rushed to help the customer struggle out of the black dress with the white sash.

The widow took a couple of deep breaths and announced her decision: "Something has to be done."

The seamstress folded up her rumpled masterpiece.

"I'll do my best", she promised, though not quite sure what for: the tight dress or the dead chairlady.

On Wednesday morning the seamstress delivered the dress, but it turned out that she had guessed wrong. The widow wanted her to see the Soubirous girl and find out what could be done for the ghost of Massabieille.

The very idea offended the young woman. Her father was assistant town clerk, she pointed out, and she herself was a Child of Mary in good standing. There could be no question of her calling on the likes of the Soubirous. As for the chairlady, she evidently needed Masses—

"I'll pay for Masses", said the widow, "if they're what she wants." And she added that as the poor soul had so far shown itself to Bernadette alone, Bernadette was the one to ask about its wishes.

"Madame," said the seamstress, and her nose looked white and as sharp as the point of a dagger, "I won't enter that filthy hovel."

Nor did she. She waited out in the alley, that evening, while the widow squeezed herself through the passage into the Old Jail, to talk to the Soubirous. The conference took a long time—or was it only the seamstress who was impatient? At last the widow reappeared, beaming. Apparently the mother had been difficult at first, but a reminder of her Christian duty had made her give in. She would send Bernadette to the grotto with the ladies on Sunday.

"Sunday?" The seamstress looked pained. "Does Madame want the whole town to see us?"

"Oh, no!" said the widow, horrified—and went right back to change the appointment. But the seamstress was tired of standing guard outside. She said good-bye; Madame could let her know what happened.

She had not yet left the alley when she heard the widow calling after her. Everything was settled, the fat woman reported when she caught up. It had not taken a minute. "The girl did it. She just said, 'Let's go tomorrow!'" marveled the widow.

Tomorrow was Thursday.

Bernadette's mother left home before dawn; she had washing to do for the schoolmistress. She felt uneasy; her sister had told her all about the schoolmistress' opinion of visions at Massabieille. And indeed they were the first subject that came up as she gathered the laundry to take it down to the river.

Louise Soubirous could not lie. Shamefacedly she admitted breaking her resolution to keep the girl away from the haunted place. "You're going to have trouble with the police", warned the schoolmistress.

The frightened mother grabbed the bundle of laundry and ran home to stop her child. She came too late, though. Bernadette was gone.

This Thursday, the eighteenth of February, was market day in Lourdes. A crowd filled the town from early morning on, and nobody paid any attention to the two women and the child on the forest road to Massabieille. The widow carried a blessed candle for safety. The seamstress had had another brilliant idea; as assistant town clerk, her father kept pen and ink at home, and she had brought those, along with a sheet of paper. She had always admired the late chairlady's handwriting; if the poor soul really chose now to be seen or heard by Bernadette alone, its writing would identify it and explain its wishes. There was no need to depend on the likes of the Soubirous, thought the clever seamstress.

The widow was panting heavily when they came to the top of the path that ran down to the grotto. The little girl had led the way faster and faster; she was swooping down the steep trail now as if she had wings. The women had a hard time getting down, especially the widow. They clutched at the shrubs and set one foot carefully in front of the other, but a few times they lost their footing all the same and had to squat in a hurry—especially the widow.

Bernadette was waiting at the bottom, opposite the niche. They took her between them, and she knelt down on a flat stone. The seamstress lit the candle, sheltered from the wind by the big rock. Bernadette's face looked blank; she impressed the seamstress as a rather common little girl and not too likable. But as she drew out her rosary now, the women did the same and knelt down to pray with her.

All of a sudden Bernadette's face lit up. Like a cry of rejoicing it came from her lips: "She's there!"

"Be quiet!" the seamstress scolded the noisy child. "Let us say the rosary." The widow nodded in agreement.

Bernadette's eyes hung blissfully on the niche. The seamstress completed the rosary and got up. "Go and ask the Lady what she wants", she ordered the child. "And ask her to write it down on the paper."

Obediently Bernadette rose, took paper, pen, and ink, and advanced a few steps without taking her eyes off the niche.

The widow got up, too, and joined the seamstress. Together, a few steps back, they started following the girl. Bernadette did not turn her head. She merely made a sign with her right hand, and the women scurried back into hiding, dropping to their knees in the underbrush beneath the great rock.

From there they could see Bernadette dutifully holding up paper, pen, and ink toward the niche. The niche appeared to be empty. Empty, too, was the paper that Bernadette brought back to them. For an instant they could see her radiant face when she took the blessed candle from the seamstress' hand. "The Lady started laughing", she said. And she was gone again.

Shocked, the women stayed on their knees. They had meant to be helpful; were they now mocked and doomed? Bernadette seemed to be far away. The two could not hear a sound, but the child knelt quite close to the niche now, her head a little atilt, up-turned as if to listen in raptured devotion.

The lovely laugh had been the first sound from her Lady; but now she opened her lips and spoke to Bernadette:

"I do not need to write what I have to say."

If she had written, Bernadette could not have read it. But now the girl understood perfectly. She under-stood every word the Lady uttered with so kind a smile—for she spoke the patois of the valley:

"I cannot promise you happiness in this world, but in another."

A shudder of bliss ran through Bernadette. The Lady asked:

"Will you do me the favor of coming here for a fortnight? It would give me pleasure."

To the waiting women it seemed as though a sigh came from Bernadette's lips, a "Yes", breathed into the wind—or did the wind alone so gently bend the briars?

The blessed candle in Bernadette's hand flickered—a tiny spark in the flood of light pouring down from the cloudless sky. Suddenly the two watchers realized that she was back between them. The seamstress was the first to recover. "Well, does she want Masses, or doesn't she?"

Bernadette was amazed. "Didn't you hear? She was speaking so clearly." And, with folded hands, she re-peated:

"I cannot promise you happiness in this world, but in another—"

"Then she can't have come from purgatory", said the widow. "On the contrary. . ." She became silent, as though afraid to say more.

"What was she asking when you said 'yes'?" asked the seamstress.

"She asked me to come here for a fortnight—"

"You're going to see her for two whole weeks?" marveled the widow.

"I said, 'I'll ask my parents' ", replied the child.

They wanted to know if they might come again.

Bernadette smiled. "The Lady looked at you for a long time. Right at the start."

"Perhaps she was looking at the candle?" the widow suggested humbly.

"No, it was you. She looked at you and smiled."

The seamstress could not imagine a spirit being so well disposed toward the widow. And what about her, a Child of Mary in good standing? "Let's go home", she said and gave the Soubirous girl a dark look. "If you're lying, God will punish you."

All unnoticed, the small blessed candle had burned down.

4

GROTTO DUTY

A CHILD WHO SEES A SPIRIT is one thing; a spirit that makes a daily date with a child for two weeks is another. Bernadette's parents felt out of their depth. Everyone gave them advice and left them more bewildered. A decision had to be made, but they were not up to it. What to do? They called a family meeting.

The family met in the Old Jail. Uncle André came down from upstairs but did not say much; he took this occasion to inspect his property. Aunt Bernarde said enough for two. The mistake, she declared at once, was that the child had gone to the grotto with two strangers, rather than with her.

"With you?" Mother wondered. "*You* said she shouldn't have gone at all!"

"But she went. So she should have gone with me", said Aunt Bernarde.

"But if it's a trap?" wailed the worried mother.

That, the godmother shrewdly observed, was a question for the girl's confessor. He had allowed it, so it could do no harm.

Mother shook her head. "You don't know what it can do. You weren't at the mill last Sunday."

"When all the brats went crazy?" Uncle André chuckled at the memory. "Served them right. Don't let it happen again, though. I don't want to hear from my customers. You fill those cracks in the floor, François—"

"I've heard enough", Father shouted. "I don't want to hear from anyone." He was thinking of the police and his own two weeks behind bars. "I'm her father, and I say let's stop it. I'm responsible—"

"That's not what they call you in town." Aunt Bernarde's voice had an edge to it. "At least those you owe money—not that I'd be uncharitable about it. Anyway, I didn't come here to discuss you, but your daughter."

Bernadette stood by the barred window. She did not look out at the manure pile. Her eyes were cast down, and her mind seemed far away until her godmother was heard again: "The Lady ordered her to come for a fortnight—"

"No", Bernadette said. "She said: 'It would give me pleasure.'"

"Did you hear that, Bernarde?" cried her mother. "Only a devil in disguise would say such a thing."

The uncle swept the younger children off the bed and peered underneath for rat marks. He had been only half listening, but he had never seen Bernadette so happy. "Calm down, Louise", he mumbled. "If it gives the little one pleasure—" Then he straightened up fast. Someone was knocking.

Father jumped as if the policemen were already there. At a sign from Mother, Bernadette went to open the door—but it was only the widow who stood in the passage. The child welcomed her with an awkward bow. The others nodded stiffly. She had come for Bernadette, said the widow.

"Again?" Mother sounded upset. "Without you, Madame, my daughter would have been through going to that—that place."

"I'm so grateful I could be along", said the widow. "I want to show my appreciation." She glanced at the pitiful surroundings. "Won't you please let her be my guest for a while?"

It would be good for Bernadette's health, Mother

thought, especially the food! Aunt Bernarde considered how few people liked the widow. But then the
fat woman proudly related her conversations of today:
the baker's wife had hardly let her go; the cobbler's
wife had come right along with her; the gendarme
sergeant had listened in, clearly impressed—

Father winced. The gendarmes kept order through-
out the land, and even the town police treated them
with great respect. François Soubirous had never been
in trouble with them.

The uncle muttered that it wouldn't be a bad idea
to send the little one elsewhere. He did not want
gendarmes snooping around his house, either.

The widow chattered on. Just now she had been
questioned by one of the postmaster's girls; she didn't
know which—

"Must have been Rosine", said the uncle. "Dominiquette's too stuck-up."

"So I told her: 'Of course she'll be going tomorrow'", said the widow.

Not without her family she wouldn't, said Aunt
Bernarde.

The postmaster's girl had impressed Mother, too.
She got Bernadette's cape and hung it around her
shoulders. "Come back early tomorrow", she said.

Bernadette waited.

Aunt Bernarde turned to Mother. "I'll get a candle.
She'll need something blessed down there."

Louise Soubirous looked desperately around. "I'll

come along, of course", she blurted out—and before she could take it back, Bernadette was gone with the widow.

Toinette and Jean, in their corner, sat and stared. At the widow's, one would never be hungry!

The widow's house was warm, as warm as the Old Jail in midsummer. More food was served for supper than Bernadette had seen in months. Afterward she was sent to sleep all alone in a huge bed that was dazzling white and softer than a haymow, but she could not close an eye. All she did was count the hours.

Before dawn she led the widow back to the Old Jail, to pick up Mother. The cobbler's wife and two or three others were waiting in the alley. The seamstress had stayed away; but from the inn Aunt Bernarde arrived to join them, with a candle.

At Massabieille Bernadette darted down the steep path again. "She'll break her neck!" cried the women, who had to help each other down on their hands and knees. But when they got to the bottom, the child was kneeling in prayer before the niche, the lighted candle in one hand, her rosary in the other.

At the third Hail Mary her face changed. There was no need for the little cry of joy that had earned her a scolding the day before. One had only to look at her now to know she was seeing the Lady. The smile that glowed and wavered and glowed again on her lips was not like an earthly smile. She bowed both with her head and with her hands—it was as though she had done nothing all her life but learn how to bow. The women could not take their eyes off her.

After about a quarter of an hour she stirred, like someone waking up. Aunt Bernarde feared she might fall. She put her arms around the girl and said, "May the good God keep us all from harm!" Mother only nodded, glad to see her child look less frightening than at the mill on Sunday. Nobody dared to ask what the Lady had said today. Turning to go, Bernadette cast a farewell glance at the niche: "Till tomorrow", she whispered blissfully.

"Till tomorrow", each of the women said at the parting of their ways. Bernadette walked with the widow, followed by curious eyes. More and more people greeted the fat woman as they saw her with the child in the dark cloak. A pretty young girl ran breathlessly after them. "I'm Rosine—who is your Lady?" she asked the child.

"I don't know. She hasn't told me", Bernadette replied.

The widow took her hand and patted it tenderly. "Anyway, it's such a joy to be there when you see our Lady", she said as they went on.

The girl gasped. Our Lady—or had it just been a slip of the widow's tongue? "Dominiquette!" she called and ran back to the corner where another, younger girl was waiting. "Dominiquette, we must go to the grotto!"

The other turned up her nose. "You go, Rosine. I wouldn't go anywhere in such company", she told her sister.

Outside her door the widow was saluted by two men in uniform. "Good morning, Sergeant", she beamed at the tall one who wore a sword and a cocked hat. Bernadette followed her into the house, without seeming to see the gendarme or his companion, the red-nosed town constable who had taken Father to jail not long ago.

They looked darkly at the door that closed behind her. "A very common child", said the gendarme. "I'll keep my eyes on that grotto."

"I'm keeping mine on the child", said the constable.

The cobbler's wife, on her way home, ran into the tax collector's sister. "Have you heard, Mademoiselle?" she began. "A girl has seen a beautiful lady, and people think it's the Blessed Virgin—or," she added quickly, seeing the other frown, "or the soul of poor Mademoiselle Elise."

Everyone in Lourdes knew how fond Mademoiselle Estrade had been of the late chairlady of the Children of Mary. She did not think it was a joking matter. "Tell your stories elsewhere", she said coldly and walked away.

I'll show you, thought the cobbler's wife, and went to tell her stories elsewhere.

On Saturday, some twenty people were waiting at

daybreak for Bernadette to come to Massabieille. The postmaster's Rosine had brought a friend; an old lady, who had heard about it from the cobbler's wife, came

with her maid; a few were carrying candles. In the background, watching quietly, stood the big gendarme.

"Here she comes", a murmur ran down the trail as Bernadette appeared on the forest road, far ahead of her mother and aunt and the widow. Her feet hardly touched the ground any more in her flight down the rock to the flat stone she used to kneel on, and she had no eyes for anything but the niche.

"Now she sees her", whispered the kneeling women.

Above, a group of quarry workers appeared and stopped to watch. One of them took off his cap. The others did the same. The last one said, "That child sees the Blessed Virgin."

What made him say it? He did not know.

Back in town, the cobbler's wife met Mademoiselle Estrade again. "It's true!" she cried. "Bernadette has seen the Blessed Virgin! I was there myself, and many others . . ."

So now they were leaving poor Elise's soul in peace and claiming instead to see the Virgin in the flesh! The tax collector and his sister lived in the same house as the chief of police. Mademoiselle went to see the chief's wife. She, too, had heard of the story. Her husband was looking into it. Of course, the grotto was out of town and the concern of the gendarmes, but the girl came from the worst family in Lourdes and certainly bore watching.

"Dreadfully poor people", sighed the chief's wife. "My little Amanda here gave the first pair of socks she ever knitted to the poorest child in town—and would you believe it? It was that girl's brother."

Mademoiselle Estrade absent-mindedly stroked little Amanda's head. She did not know that the poor boy was the same she had caught nibbling candle wax in church; but she felt strangely touched. "Will you keep me informed?" she asked her friend.

"But of course, my dear", promised the chief's wife.

That evening, the red-nosed constable brought his chief two interesting reports. First, he said, Bernadette Soubirous had left the widow's house, where she had been pampered since Thursday, and gone back to her parents.

"What?" thundered the chief. "Then they must be after bigger game. We'll find out soon enough what their scheme is. And what else?"

And the major commanding the gendarmes of the whole province had come to town, to see what went on at the grotto. He had left his horse and escort at the Citadel and was now dining at the hotel, said the constable.

The chief rubbed his hands. "Fine. That's fine. Go and give the major my compliments. If he takes care of the grotto, I'll put a stop to this business here in Lourdes."

"Yes, sir", said the constable and headed for the hotel.

So the major, shown to Massabieille on Sunday morning by his sergeant and the constable, was not surprised to see a fair-sized crowd around a child who simply knelt on a stone, staring at a rock. The major, ten paces away, saw nothing. He thought there was nothing. And yet, he did not feel like making fun of the child. When she got up, he asked, "Did you see anything?"

Bernadette had ceased to wonder at such questions. She knew by then that others could not see or hear the Lady, no matter how lovely she was, how plainly she spoke. "Yes," she said, "I saw her. She spoke to me."

The major nodded. "Has your chief seen this?" he asked the constable.

"Oh, he wouldn't look at anything like that, sir!"

"Hmm", said the major. Later, when his horse was brought from the Citadel, he told his sergeant to have a man at the grotto every morning. "Report to me daily what is said and done, and how many people are present."

"Yes, sir. Is that all, sir?"

"That's all", said the major and rode away.

The sergeant spat on the ground. "Something new", he said disdainfully. "Grotto duty!"

On that Sunday, Louise Soubirous went to vespers with her children. At the church door, they passed the postmaster's girls. Dominiquette peered over a moment and then swept right past the disreputable family, but Rosine ran up to Bernadette and hugged her. "What did the Lady say today?" she asked under her breath.

Bernadette shook her head. It was a secret.

"Oh", said the girl, disappointed. "What's the use of a secret if you mustn't tell?"

Bernadette smiled. "Don't worry, it'll be very useful to me", she said. Then she followed the others into the twilight of the old church.

After vespers, walking out beside Toinette, she heard two men's voices.

"There she is."

"Which one?"

"That one."

The glare of the afternoon sun was still in her eyes when a hand fell on her arm, and the second voice said, "Follow me." It was the chief of police.

"Wherever you wish, Monsieur", the child said obediently.

From the steps, her mother and sister looked after her in dumb horror. The chief wore plain clothes, but, even so, he was an awesome figure; they said in Lourdes that in his full-dress uniform you could mistake him for a general. But Bernadette seemed not afraid as she walked behind him, with the constable bringing up the rear.

The crowd in the square made way for the odd little procession. Women muttered, "Isn't he wicked?" Some started sobbing. "Poor Bernadette," cried one, "they'll put you in prison!"

"I'm not scared", she called back. "If they put me in, they'll let me out again."

The chief frowned and continued silently to his house. There, too, he caused some excitement. His wife rapped at the Estrades' door: "They're bringing her in for questioning", she said importantly. And as she scurried back to her husband's office, she found the constable peeping through the keyhole.

"Well!" she said and cleared her throat. The constable fled in embarrassment. Then the lady peeped through the keyhole.

The child sat facing her husband across the large desk. A ragged cape hid most of her thin face. Her hands lay clasped on her knees. Her head was bent forward, as if straining to understand. The chief's wife was doing the same at her keyhole, when the two Estrades came down the hall and she had to straighten up in a hurry.

"Coming in, Madame?" the tax collector asked courteously. When she said she was not interested, he expressed sympathy. "I should not have come, either, if my dear sister hadn't pulled my arm, taken my chair away, and practically pushed me over here."

The chief's wife laughed. "Well, now you can watch my husband triumph over a silly peasant girl." She cautiously opened the door and waved them both in.

They sat down quietly in a corner. Bernadette took no notice, but the chief, as though egged on by their presence, raised his voice: "You say it's the Blessed Virgin who has appeared to you?"

Bernadette shook her head. "I don't know. She hasn't told me."

"Very well", he agreed. "Then someone else has told you that you've seen the Blessed Virgin. Do you know who it was?"

Bernadette's voice sounded hoarse. "No, Monsieur."

The chief wrote on a piece of paper. "You see," he said, "I'll write down whatever you wish. If you tell the truth, I'll know it—but be careful to tell me no lies! Look here, you'd better admit right now that you lied, if you don't want to go to jail. Go on. Speak."

"I didn't lie to you, Monsieur", the child answered.

He began reading the notes he had jotted down. "The Lady wore golden shoes—"

"I didn't say that, Monsieur", she broke in quickly.

"You did", he thundered.

Bernadette kept calm. "The dress and the roses hide everything but her toes. That's what I said."

She did not get flustered, although the chief's tone grew more and more threatening. "You made a mistake", she repeated. He kept twisting her words around, glaring, and shouting at her. He even raised his hand, so that Mademoiselle Estrade in her corner gave a start. He was so angry that when he wanted to dip his pen, he could not find the inkwell.

"What do you think?" Mademoiselle whispered to her brother.

"The child is in good faith", he whispered back.

"She may have been fooled. But there is something extraordinary behind her story."

At this instant, the door at Bernadette's back opened. A man's head appeared. "What do you want?" roared the chief.

"Monsieur, I—I'm the father of the child—"

"Ah", said the chief, rubbing his hands. "It's you, Soubirous. I was just going to send for you. This nonsense with your girl has got to stop. It's upsetting the peace of the town. I warn you: if you haven't enough authority to keep her home, I have plenty to shut her up elsewhere."

"I understand, Monsieur." Father eagerly twisted his beret in his hands. "I'll be frank, Monsieur. We didn't dare turn people away, so far, but since you say so, I'll keep my door shut. And you can be sure my child won't go to Massabieille again."

Bernadette's shoulders drooped. But the chief was content. He dismissed the pair, and when they got home, Father said they would all be put in jail if the girl went back to the grotto.

Mother sobbed and wrung her hands. "Don't you go there again—you hear me? Don't ever go near that place again!"

Bernadette stared at the cracked stone floor. "Then I must disobey either you or the Lady", she said helplessly.

Early on Monday, the road to the grotto was dotted with expectant groups of women. The schoolmistress argued with some outside the Old Jail. "What are you waiting for?" she asked them. "Bernadette can't go. Her mother promised me she wouldn't let her."

"Who are you to keep the child from her duty?" asked the cobbler's wife. "She was told to come for a fortnight."

"Will you go to jail for her then?" the schoolmistress snapped back. She made her way through the crowd and returned after a while, leading Bernadette by the hand. "I'll take her to her catechism class, where she belongs", she announced, and the others went home grumbling.

On Mondays the class was taught by the Mother Superior. She received Bernadette with a scolding. Why had she not been here a week ago?

Bernadette's eyes were on the floor. "My mother thought I was sick, Reverend Mother."

"I see. I thought perhaps you had another engagement."

The children giggled. They were all younger than Bernadette and enjoyed feeling above her. When all were present, a bell rang for prayers. "Hail Mary, full of grace . . ."

A quick longing flooded Bernadette's heart. "Pray for us sinners", she said with the rest of them. Like the rest, she made the Sign of the Cross, but her hand felt heavy. Would Mother let her go in the afternoon?

The Mother Superior's voice cut through her thoughts. "We shall recite the Confiteor. I confess to

Almighty God—" She broke off and thrust out her chin at Bernadette. "Continue!"

Bernadette got up. "To blessed Mary, ever Virgin—to blessed . . ." She hung her head.

"You don't know your saints, but you claim to have visions", sneered the Mother Superior. "If you do see the Blessed Virgin, ask her to teach you the catechism that you find so difficult to learn. Now kneel and repeat ten times: Through my fault, through my most grievous fault . . ."

On her way home for noon recess, Bernadette stopped to ask the chaplain what to do. "They have no right to keep you from going", he replied.

At home, however, Mother brought up Father's promise to the police chief. Bernadette was sent back to school. Obediently, she trudged along until she was in sight of the hospice. There, she suddenly stopped. An invisible barrier seemed to have risen in front of her; for an instant she could not move at all. Then an irresistible force turned her around, toward a shortcut to the river and the bridge that led to Massabieille.

It was a country lane passing between the town and the Citadel. Not many people took this road, as a rule, and yet the little girl in the dark cloak had hardly set foot on it when half of Lourdes was astir. Children playing at the edge of town saw her first. "She's going!" they yelled and ran to see what would happen; "Bernadette is going to the grotto!"

Within seconds, people were pouring out of houses and rushing in from the fields for the sensation.

"Bring me my godmother's candle", Bernadette said to the first who caught up with her. "I need it."

A few children dashed off. The rest stayed with Bernadette. The crowd kept growing; soon it numbered about a hundred. At their approach the gates of the Citadel opened, and the sergeant came out with another gendarme. He was all set to stop them, but then he remembered his orders; he was to watch and report on the goings-on at the grotto—that was all. He motioned to his companion, and, with the child between them, they went on grotto duty.

At the main road the children who had run to the inn came back, and after them Aunt Bernarde, out of breath and carrying her blessed candle. The sergeant looked disgusted. "To think this is the nineteenth century, and we're asked to believe such superstitious nonsense!" he said in a loud voice.

Mademoiselle Estrade—who was there with a friend and kept well in the rear of the crowd—raised the collar of her fur wrap a bit higher and hung back a little farther. The ladies were the last to reach the grotto. They found Bernadette already kneeling. Her hand with the candle was somewhat shaky today. The gendarmes stood beside her, watching closely. The people waited. Many prayed. Bernadette's face did not change.

The sergeant followed her gaze, took a close look at the niche, and shrugged his shoulders. "Do you see her?" the other gendarme asked the child.

Bernadette shook her head. She pointed at the sergeant; the move made her candle flicker and die. "That officer stands there—I can't see anything", she murmured wretchedly.

The sergeant laughed, but one could see his annoyance. "If I look like the Devil, at least I'm a pretty good devil", he said and strode back to her side. "If you weren't a little idiot, you would know the Blessed Virgin isn't scared of the police."

Bernadette stared at the niche.

The sergeant stroked his mustache and tapped her on the shoulder. "And why are you scared? Maybe it's because you're a little liar?"

A few people snickered. Others were angry. Only Mademoiselle Estrade was stunned. "Look," she whispered in her friend's ear, "she simply admits that she didn't see anything!"

Unsteadily, Bernadette got up and walked away. Aunt Bernarde took her arm and led her through the disappointed crowd to the mill. There they made her sit down in the kitchen again, and again her mother burst in soon, full of rage and worry and reproaches.

Bernadette looked up. Her eyes were dry, too deeply hurt for tears. "Mamma", she said, almost inaudibly. "I don't know how I failed her . . ."

It broke her mother's heart. She knew it was her fault if the Lady was angry. "I'll never meddle again", Louise cried and threw her arms around her child.

5

HEARTBURN

THE CHILDREN of Lourdes went into huddles. "The Lady's a fraidycat", they chanted. "She beat it from the police."

The mothers heard it from the children and told it to the fathers. Before nightfall, the new joke had made the round of taverns and cafés. "That old fox of a police chief has only to stick his nose in, and the Lady makes herself scarce and goes looking for another rock—ha, ha!"

The old fox did not care whom he scared, the child or the Lady. It did not matter which of them stayed away, just so there were no more meetings. Of course, the police would have to keep an eye on everything—Old Jail and grotto, children and grown-ups. That, after all, was what the police were for.

The chief's wife confided to Mademoiselle Estrade that the "seer", as they called Bernadette, was expected to make a last try next morning. The tax collector's sister felt an urge to see the child again. But how? She talked it over with her friends. They were as curious as she was and as willing to get up at dawn, for once. But for ladies to go unescorted to a place like Massabieille, at such an hour, was out of the question. "You must ask your brother to go with us", they told Mademoiselle Estrade.

She promised to try. Had he not been clearly impressed by the girl's conduct under questioning? Mademoiselle, who managed her brother's household, set the stage by ordering his favorite dish, fresh brook trout, for dinner and by preparing the sauce herself, from their grandmother's recipe.

After one trout, the tax collector of Lourdes looked up at the ceiling, pursed his lips, and dreamily said, "Ah—!"

His sister took heart and casually mentioned that she and her friends wished to go to the grotto tomorrow. He started to grin at once, which made things difficult. "We'll have to go early", she said, "if we want to see well."

"The show is a hit, eh?" He almost split his sides laughing.

She almost swallowed a fish bone. "Of course not! I mean, it's not like a show at all. It just wouldn't be right for ladies to go alone, before sunup."

"I daresay it wouldn't. Who's the moron you want to go with you?"

There went her chance . . . "But look, dear—you said yourself she's in good faith", she faltered.

"I?" A light dawned on him. "I said she may have been fooled. But I don't care to see her fool a lot of others, least of all such morons." Monsieur Estrade had lost his appetite. He folded his napkin, and there was something final about the way he laid it down. "I don't share your interest in the matter, and I will not make myself ridiculous. By the way, I thought the police closed that show."

Mademoiselle was unable to take his no for an answer. He had always been so good-natured and easy to handle! "They've no right to keep her from going", she argued. "The little chaplain thought so, too."

Her brother preferred not to say what he thought of the chaplain. He was fed up with all that nonsense. He would have coffee at the café, he declared. "Good night, my dear. See you tomorrow."

Walking out, he caught her eye, and the disappointment in it stung him. He was hardly in the street when he started wavering. At the café he would have to hear similar nonsense. Should he go home and make up? No. Not so fast, anyway. Those priests! he thought. Were they really going along with all this?

Without intending to, he turned in the direction of the church. He really was not much of a church-going man—religious activities were his sister's department—but from time to time he liked to call on the Curé Peyramale. As parish priest of Lourdes, Father Peyramale was the little chaplain's superior. He was straightforward and had a good deal of common sense. A frank word with him could do no harm, thought the tax collector.

He found the Curé in the sacristy. The gray-haired priest was a striking figure of a man; with his power-ful body hunched in a chair, he looked more than ever like an old mountain eagle. It was a pleasure to see Monsieur Estrade in church, even for a social chat, he said amiably.

He had come for advice, explained the visitor. And, with the faintly belittling smile of a man of the world, he briefly outlined his sister's curious notion. What could be done about it?

The priest furrowed his brow.

"I see no harm in doing what your sister asks", he replied in his deep, ringing voice. "In your place, I should have gone before now. I agree with you that there probably is nothing in it but a child's delusions.

But I don't think your dignity would suffer from going to see a thing that takes place in broad daylight and is the talk of the town."

Monsieur Estrade was surprised. Of course, there was no reason why he should not go to Massabieille. But was there a reason why he should?

The Curé nodded. "I should be glad if some reliable people went and saw what goes on there." And as the other man seemed unable to make up his mind, he added, with sudden firmness, "Yes, do go with the ladies."

That was an order. Father Peyramale considered no refusal and would tolerate none. On his way home, half-peeved and half-amused, the tax collector kept thinking: Well, I asked for it.

Thus it happened that the break of dawn on Tuesday found him grotto-bound at the head of a squad of ladies. He felt pretty silly, having to shepherd this solemn group through the town, and on the forest road he began to poke fun at them. Did they have their opera glasses with them? Were they well supplied with holy water? Had one of them brought a candle? The ladies giggled—all but his sister, who tried in vain to put them into a more serious mood.

It was in this frame of mind that Monsieur Estrade first came upon the cave of Massabieille, where they used to take the pigs. Bernadette had not yet arrived, but a hundred and fifty or two hundred people were there before him and his company. Many women were on their knees, and the tax collector found it hard to keep from laughing at the childish belief of these simple Christians.

He recovered some of his wounded pride when he found that the crowd included other gentlemen of Lourdes. Directly in front of the grotto he saw three of them: the town's leading lawyer, the commander of the garrison of soldiers in the Citadel, and the owner of the sawmill. It was in his meadow that three children had looked for firewood not quite two weeks ago and started all this commotion. The three gentlemen began to explore the grotto. Monsieur Estrade joined them. They found nothing worthy of note.

The church bells in town struck seven, the hour when Bernadette used to come after morning Mass. A confused murmur ran through the crowd. The gentlemen heard someone try to clear a path for Bernadette. The ranks opened, and the child appeared with a woman whom the tax collector recognized: she kept a cheap inn in the town.

The gentlemen elbowed their way through to Bernadette's side and prepared to observe her. She knelt down, took her rosary out of her pocket, and made a deep bow. It struck Monsieur Estrade that she did it all without the slightest awkwardness or self-consciousness, just as simply as if she had gone into the parish church for her ordinary devotions. While the beads passed through her fingers, she kept her eyes on the rock as though waiting for something.

The crowd waited with her. But they were all looking at her, not at the niche. She had just finished the first decade of her rosary when a smile seemed to interrupt her prayers for a moment. It was a smile unlike anything Monsieur Estrade had ever seen. A light shone in her eyes; an indescribable grace seemed to change her whole being. Bernadette, he thought, was no longer Bernadette; she was one of those privileged few whose features radiate the glory of heaven.

And without giving another thought to his dignity, Monsieur Estrade took off his hat and knelt down, just like the humblest peasant woman. He saw nothing; he heard nothing. But he knew there was a conversation taking place between the mysterious Lady and the child before his eyes.

When the Lady spoke, a thrill of joy seemed to grip the girl's body. When the girl made a request, she would bow down to the ground and be moved almost to tears. She seemed afraid to lower her eyes, afraid even for an instant to lose sight of her enchanting vision. Monsieur Estrade saw her make the Sign of the Cross and knew that if this sign was made in heaven, it must be made there as Bernadette made it.

A last radiant glow lit up her face, and then—so gradual that it was almost unnoticeable—the transfiguring glory of her ecstasy grew fainter and disappeared. She went on praying for a few more moments, but now the tax collector saw nothing but the face of a little peasant girl.

A little peasant girl lost herself in the crowd before his eyes, and a crowd of disturbing thoughts invaded his mind. He had felt the presence of the Lady in the grotto; he was unable to talk about it with the ladies he had accompanied to the spot. When his sister looked for him, he was gone.

That day's vision had lasted for a full hour. Back in town, Mademoiselle Estrade went to the parish church. The door of the sacristy was open; inside, the Curé was pacing up and down. When he caught sight of her, he came out to ask whether her brother had been to the grotto, and what he thought of the whole thing.

"My brother was at the grotto," she replied, "but I can hardly say what he thought. I haven't seen him since the child came out of her ecstasy."

"I expect he'll come to see me", said the Curé.

In a dark corner of the church, alone before the Blessed Virgin, knelt Monsieur Estrade. "When at the last great hour I must appear before thy Divine Son," he prayed, "vouchsafe to be my protectress and to remember that thou hast seen me on my knees in thy grotto at Lourdes, when thou didst reveal thyself to Bernadette, and through Bernadette to me."

Mademoiselle Estrade's longing to see Bernadette again became so strong that she could not await the next day. On that same afternoon, before the sun set over Massabieille, she went to the Soubirous address. It had been described to her but, when she actually saw the dilapidated hovel at the foot of the fortress walls, she thought she had gone wrong after all.

A small boy squatted in the mud outside the door, playing with colored pebbles. He threw them against the moldy wall and caught them when they bounced back. "Little boy," the lady called from a safe distance, "can you tell me where Bernadette Soubirous lives?"

He looked up, surprised. The tax collector's sister recognized the child she had seen eating candle wax in church and had fed at her back door. "Don't I know you?" she asked.

The boy tried to hide his face.

"Well!" she said. "Why didn't you come back to the house?"

He scratched his hair. It was filthy. "Mother won't let me", he said at last. "She says we mustn't go begging."

There was a pause.

"Do you know Bernadette?" the lady asked, more cautiously.

The boy gulped. "She—she's my sister."

Mademoiselle winced and looked away. She ought not to have come here, she thought; it was too much for her nerves. Now the little boy brought up a small, scrawny, dirty hand to point at a second-story window: "She's staying upstairs now. Our uncle took her up, because so many people come to look at her."

Mademoiselle felt embarrassed. "Thank you", she

said and entered the dark hallway. She groped her way up a flight of creaking stairs and knocked on a door at the top. It was opened. Behind it was a fairly clean room.

A ray of late sunlight fell through the window on Bernadette, who sat with a very small child in her lap. She tried to get up, but the child seemed too stiff to be lifted easily, so she only nodded in greeting. Mademoiselle Estrade went over and introduced herself. "I know you", she said.

The man who had opened the door withdrew. Bernadette rocked the child in her arms. It looked oddly lifeless, almost like a wax doll. "Another brother of yours?" asked the visiting lady.

The girl shook her head. "It belongs to a neighbor. I'm only minding it while she gets the doctor. It's sick."

This was obvious. But somehow it was a relief to know that the wretched creature was at least no brother of Bernadette's.

"My baby brother is downstairs with my parents", said the girl. She looked questioningly at a rickety sofa. If Mademoiselle would like to sit down—?

Mademoiselle preferred to stand. She did not want to stay long, anyhow. The questions she had intended asking stuck in her throat. Poor child, was all she could think—poor child! And of course she meant Bernadette, not the whimpering infant.

Then the stairs creaked and groaned again, and the

doctor appeared in the door, with a haggard-looking woman. He headed straight for the lady. "Mademoiselle, you here? What a surprise!"

A sense of shame overcame her. "You attend to your patient, Doctor", she said quickly. "I'd only be in the way. I'll wait downstairs."

Out in the alley again, she drew a few deep breaths. Bernadette's brother had vanished. A single lost, colored pebble lay at the bottom of the old prison wall. Mademoiselle Estrade walked up and down. The doctor, she thought, ought to see Bernadette at the grotto. He wouldn't recognize her!

In a matter of minutes, the doctor came out with his black bag. "I didn't keep you waiting too long, did I? Nothing to be done for that child. The mother—she's the woman who cleans the streets, you know—won't believe it's a hopeless case. Complete palsy. He'll live another month or two, at the most. May I see you home, Mademoiselle?"

She accepted gladly. "Do you know Bernadette, Doctor?"

He nodded. Another case one could do little about. No acute danger, but not much chance of curing that asthma, either. It was probably tuberculosis, and no wonder, in these conditions. "Medicine can't work miracles", the doctor concluded.

Yes, it was all very sad, the lady agreed. Had the doctor seen the child at the grotto?

"I, Mademoiselle?" The doctor blinked through his

glasses. He was too busy for children's games. He had a patient waiting at every corner, so to speak. "See the stone-cutter's sign up there? His optic nerve is paralyzed. Amaurosis, we call it. In a few weeks the man will go blind on me. Then the sign will come down, too."

Medical case histories upset Mademoiselle Estrade. She was glad to be near home. Just as she turned to thank the doctor, her brother came down the street. He raised his hat to her and also turned to the doctor.

"Glad to see you, old man. You'll have to do me a favor."

"Heartburn again? Charcoal and fennel tea, three times a day after meals", the doctor said helpfully.

The tax collector shook his head. No, he had no heartburn. At least not the kind the doctor knew how to treat. What he meant to ask concerned a poor little girl here, Bernadette Soubirous—

"What a coincidence", said the doctor. "Mademoiselle and I are just coming from her home."

"Her home?" Monsieur looked displeased. "You'd better see her at Massabieille."

"Just what I was saying", his sister threw in. He ignored her. "In fact, Doctor, I wish you'd go tomorrow. I want you to see Bernadette at the grotto and find out whether or not she is quite normal. I don't doubt it, but with all this talk about hysteria and such, I would appreciate your professional opinion."

"Well." The doctor straightened the glasses on his

nose. That put a different light on the matter, of course. Put it in the line of duty, so to speak. A diagnosis at the grotto. "I'll be there tomorrow", he promised.

"I'm sorry I can't join you", sighed the tax collector. "I'll have to leave town on business. I deeply regret it."

"It must be an interesting show", said the doctor.

Monsieur Estrade looked at him. "The only people I know who call it a show are those who haven't seen it."

Mademoiselle did not trust her ears. What had happened to her brother?

"They say the girl is acting", he went on. "In that case, she'd be the finest actress in the world. I have seen great stage stars at Toulouse and at Bordeaux; they were magnificent, but nothing like Bernadette. No, my dear Doctor. Bernadette isn't acting. She sees and hears and talks with a supernatural being."

"Hmm", said the doctor. He did not want to get into an argument with the tax collector, but supernatural beings were a bit hard to take, for a man of science.

Mademoiselle asked Monsieur whether he had seen the Curé.

"I'll go to vespers and see him then", he replied.

Her brother at vespers! Would wonders never cease?

6

MUDDY WATER

A T SIX A.M. on Wednesday the nearsighted doctor
arrived at Massabieille, carrying a lantern to see
better in the graying dawn. A number of women
were already there, among them the schoolmistress,
who no sooner set eyes on him than she came over
for a chat.

"I was the first one here today", she admitted with a kind of bashful pride. "I wanted to come yesterday. Then I felt ridiculous and went to Mass—but when I got back my maid said all the neighbors had gone. So I said, 'I'm off', but by the time I got here the vision was about over; I just saw the child smiling and bowing with such grace that I said to myself: here is something extraordinary—"

She ran out of breath. The doctor examined his lantern. "Where does she stand?" he wanted to know.

"She doesn't stand. She kneels", corrected the schoolmistress, pointing at the flat stone that was slowly being hemmed in by spectators. "Always in the same spot, right there—"

"Excuse me", the doctor said and went to greet Mademoiselle Estrade, who came down the path with the lawyer and his wife. A moment later the postmaster's two daughters arrived and joined the group.

"Dominiquette wouldn't believe me; but now that your brother says the same thing, she's all excited", Rosine complained to Mademoiselle Estrade.

"Men are so much more persuasive, my dear", Mademoiselle sighed.

Dominiquette's eyes sparkled. "I'm not excited at all", she declared. "Not at all. I'm just curious. My, what a crowd!"

The doctor returned the salutes of the gendarme sergeant and the constable. The constable seemed distressed. "Chief wants me to stop it, Doctor", he muttered unhappily.

The doctor shook his head. "Not today, my good man. Today I must examine her. Give the chief my regards; he can always stop it tomorrow."

Relieved, the constable watched the doctor take the ladies through the human wall. They did not have to wait much longer. Already Bernadette's impatient voice was heard at the foot of the steep path: "Let me through—let me through!" She certainly was in a hurry to see her illusion, the doctor thought.

He could just get to her side before she sank to her knees. Most of the crowd knelt too. The sky over the eastern mountains brightened. The doctor put down his lamp; the others raised their candles. A breeze moved the trees and blew out the candles now and then, and, whenever that happened, Bernadette held out hers to her aunt, who would relight it. The doctor drew out his handkerchief, wiped his glasses, and closely watched the girl's hands. They seemed quite steady. Her breath came evenly, too.

I must concentrate, the doctor thought as he tried to remember all the signs of hysteria. He took out his watch, reached for the hand in which the child held her rosary, and started counting the pulse beats on her wrist. They were normal and remained so for a full minute. He put his watch in his pocket. Then he seemed to have missed a change in the girl, for he heard a woman sob and another sigh, "The poor darling!"

"What do you think you see, my little joker?" said a gruff voice.

The doctor looked up, startled, and saw the sergeant reaching for Bernadette. He angrily waved the man back. Then, curious himself, he approached the niche the girl was staring at and moved the branches of the rose bush. Perhaps there was something behind it?

There was nothing. But when the doctor turned around again, he saw Bernadette sway as though about to faint. Her aunt had to support her. "She's dying", cried one of the women.

The doctor quickly counted her pulse once more. Perfectly normal, he thought; nobody is crazy but these people . . . The girl's hand slipped out of his. She got up to enter the grotto, as if looking for something. Her cheeks were pale, and two tears seemed glued to them, although she was now smiling. The doctor observed her face. It lit up and darkened and lit up again, as though clouds were passing over it. But those, of course, were the shadows of the poplars moving in the wind, for the sun had risen in the meantime.

With the crucifix of her rosary Bernadette made a slow, encompassing Sign of the Cross. The doctor heard the schoolmistress gasp, "It's upside down", but he was no expert in cross-making. His patient was all right. When she came to, it was as if she were waking from a beautiful dream, but she seemed quite like herself otherwise.

"Did I frighten you?" he asked her.

She nodded. "When you moved the branches. I was afraid you'd make the Lady fall, because her feet were resting on the rosebush."

The hallucination must be very lifelike, the doctor thought with an understanding smile. He signaled the sergeant to keep quiet—in vain. "You saw the Lady as much as I did", growled the big gendarme.

Bernadette did not reply. But suddenly Dominiquette confronted the sergeant. "This child sees, or she believes that she sees", said the postmaster's daughter.

The sergeant grinned, saluted, and made way for the schoolmistress who demanded, "Who taught you to cross yourself like that?"

"Nobody", Bernadette said. "The Lady crosses herself, and I do as she does."

That did not satisfy the schoolmistress. "How does she talk to you? In French?"

Bernadette had to laugh—a happy little laugh. "Oh, now, why should she talk French to me, Mademoiselle? Do I know French? She talks patois."

"And how come we don't hear her?"

For a moment Bernadette looked surprised again. Then she grew thoughtful. "Sometimes I think I hear her—here", she said, and pointed at her heart.

Dominiquette impulsively bent down and kissed her.

They had to go now, Aunt Bernarde said, as the

schoolmistress got ready to ask more questions. Rosine came up, too, amazed to see her sister kiss the child with the worst background in town. "You get some rest now," Dominiquette told the little one, "and don't worry. We're all for you."

"I don't worry", Bernadette said, leaving with her godmother.

"What do you think, Doctor?" asked the schoolmistress. "Was she just trying to impress us?"

The medical man shook his head. "She wasn't even aware of us. It's a genuine hallucination, but quite unhysterical."

Then they both heeded the call of duty, with the schoolmistress hurrying to class and the doctor to his next patient, the stone-cutter who was going blind.

Dominiquette looked after him. "Hallucination!" she said to Rosine. "Why don't we ask a really good doctor?"

The doctor's story angered the chief of police. Now the whole thing was back in his lap, and yet he seemed somehow unable to keep up with it. In the evening his troublesome neighbors, the Estrades, came again and pestered his wife to go with them to the grotto. "Once you've seen Bernadette in ecstasy, Madame, you will believe as we do", the tax collector assured her. The chief had to let her go.

Thursday's weather was wretched, but neither the cold drizzle nor the slushy roads kept the curious away. Nearly four hundred of them tramped in pitch-darkness to Massabieille. At seven o'clock, when only a spotted gray veil of low clouds still covered sky and mountains, the chief's wife was shocked to hear the constable yell at the top of his lungs: "Stand back! Bernadette is here!" Instead of keeping an eye on the little cheat, the fellow served her as official escort!

Despite herself, the chief's wife felt a twinge of curiosity about the surpassing loveliness that everyone said would descend on this common child. Before going into her act, the little "seer" glanced at her audience, touched her hand to her kerchief as though to arrange it more becomingly, and lifted her skirt so as not to dirty it, before kneeling down. On the police chief's wife these actions made a big impression. Three-quarters of the audience also were on their knees. The constable, though on duty, took off his cap and knelt, when he did not have to stem the surging crowd. When it rained harder and some people put up umbrellas, everyone shouted, "Umbrellas down!" and that was the last the chief's wife saw of them. She wondered what the world was coming to.

All these days she had heard about Bernadette's transformation. She looked intently but saw nothing: no gentle tears, no heavenly smile, nothing but a child who stared at a hole in the rock. After a while the child moved off on her knees, up the steep slope to the cave. At its entrance, she paused a moment, turned, and came down again on her knees, over the stony ground in the direction of the river. Suddenly she stopped, as if called by someone, looked around in obvious confusion, and slid back up, into deep mud inside the grotto.

The spectators were utterly bewildered. They saw her halt her knee-crawl at a spot where some green sprigs grew out of the mud. They saw her hand her candle to the woman beside her and, always looking and listening toward the niche, begin to dig in the wet mud with her bare hands. Three times she brought some of it to her lips and tried to gulp it down. The fourth time she swallowed it.

Horror and disgust swept the crowd. The next thing Bernadette did was to smear mud all over her face, with both hands. Then she quickly ripped off some of the green grass and swallowed that. "She's mad!" cried the wife of the police chief.

The girl took back her candle and moved out of the cave on her knees, down the steep slope, pausing several times to kiss the ground. "She's mad", repeated many voices.

For a few more moments Bernadette stayed on her knees and let a woman wipe the mud off her face. Then, abruptly, she got up and took the path back to Lourdes, without bothering about the crowd.

Laughter and jeers rang after her, and after her relatives who disappeared behind her. "You want me to believe that *that* girl sees the Blessed Virgin?" the chief's wife asked the Estrades, in a loud voice.

"Nothing was as it used to be", moaned Mademoiselle. Her brother pressed his hand to his forehead. "I'm all confused", he murmured. "I don't know what to think about it."

"You'd have done better to leave me at home", said the chief's wife. "I had little enough faith in this before; now I have less. Do you see what you've gained by dragging me out?"

They took her home and found the police chief waiting. "Well," he said in mock expectancy, "did you see the Lady?"

"Oh, yes!" His wife burst into peals of laughter. "Not a doubt of it: the Blessed Virgin has come from heaven to ask Mademoiselle Soubirous to be so gracious as to visit her at Massabieille!"

In the church of Lourdes the Curé worried about the threatened disgrace to his parish.

Father Peyramale had hoped to stay aloof, but the thing had gone too far. A muddied child led his parishioners to pray at a place of ill repute rather than before the holy altar of his church. Today the Lord had opened their eyes; it was now up to the Curé to open those of the unfortunate girl. He sent the chaplain for her.

Bernadette was frightened when she got the message. She dreaded the parish priest far more than the police. The police, after all, could only put you in jail, but what if it should be the Curé's word against the Lady's? Bernadette was not sure whether she had really done today what the Lady had meant her to do. It was some comfort to have her godmother along, but Aunt Bernarde wisely remained in the background with the chaplain when the Curé told Bernadette to step forward.

She obeyed, and his massive figure rose threateningly. "Aren't you ashamed of your conduct today at Massabieille?" he thundered. "What was the idea?"

"I don't know", she said simply. "I did what the Lady told me to."

His eagle's eye seemed to seek to pierce her soul. "Well?"

Bernadette's hands were clasped. "She said to go and drink at the spring", she explained. "I didn't see any, so I went to drink at the river. She told me it wasn't there and pointed with her finger to show me the place. I went there, but I saw only a little dirty water."

"So you drank that?"

Bernadette nodded. "The Lady said to me: 'Go and drink at the spring and wash in it.' Then she said: 'Go and eat of the plant you will find there.'"

"And you ate that grass, like an animal!" the priest burst out. "Did you not feel the humiliation of it?"

The child met his eyes without flinching. "Is that what we feel when we eat salad, Father?"

Her confessor in his corner could hardly keep back a smile. But the quaking godmother only saw the

Curé's temper rising. "You are stubborn, Bernadette Soubirous", he said icily. "Who does your Lady think she is?"

Bernadette shook her head. "I don't know. She hasn't told me."

"You don't know!" Father Peyramale was at the end of his patience. "You certainly don't! You don't know; you have no idea—you must be a fool."

Humbly Bernadette bowed her head. "Yes, Father, I'm a fool."

So the Curé dismissed her and forbade the chaplain and all other priests under his control to go near Massabieille.

Meanwhile, rain kept falling all through that Thursday, the twenty-fifth of February, 1858. It fell on the steeple of the parish church of Lourdes and on the lowly Old Jail at the foot of the Citadel. It seeped into the mud at Massabieille, where a few women and children were still on their knees. The grown-ups asked the Virgin to bring Bernadette to her senses; but one girl, not much older than Bernadette herself, wept and prayed for her father who was going blind. And the drops from on high seemed to mingle with her tears.

It was this girl who suddenly got up and cried, "Look!" pointing into the grotto. All eyes followed her finger. It pointed at the spot where Bernadette had dug in the mud.

The small hole she had made was full of water.

The little band knelt down again on the rain-soaked ground and went on praying. The next time they looked up, the hole had overflowed. A tiny stream trickled down between the stones, toward the river. And the people ran back to town to tell what they had seen.

When the stone-cutter's daughter came home, it was still daylight—but not for her father. He could not see her, though he recognized her steps. "Where have you been so long?" he asked and held out his hand.

Her eyes were full of tears that he could not see. His condition had grown steadily worse. So she took his hand and sat by his side and told him what had happened at the grotto in the morning, and of the water that trickled out of it now.

"If you go tomorrow," he said, "take a bottle and bring me some of that water."

"It's just muddy water, Papa", said the girl.

"That doesn't matter, if the Blessed Virgin sent it", her father replied.

Many who had come to market spent that night in Lourdes, to go to Massabieille with the townspeople. From nearby villages, too, small groups arrived at the grotto long before dawn. It was still raining. More and more people poured down the steep trail. They went to stare at the water, now flowing visibly from a small basin that had taken shape overnight; they crowded along the river bank, covered the top and sides of the rock, and clung to the shrubs. The gendarmes counted eight hundred—twice as many as the day before.

Among those who accompanied Bernadette from town, that Friday, was Monsieur Estrade. He came alone with the shabby crowd of the poor, who had been waiting hours at the Old Jail for the child of the poorest of them, the luckless Soubirous. No one noticed the tax collector, and he, in turn, saw nothing but Bernadette.

She was so radiant today in greeting the Lady, so full of joy! Was it the sight of the spring that caused those little bursts of childlike laughter? But what was the grief that so quickly clouded her face? Trembling and bowing, Bernadette began to climb on her knees again, kissing the ground as she went. Monsieur Estrade felt her every move in his own limbs. "Penance!" her bruised knees seemed to cry out to him at each painful step, "penance! penance!"

At the top of the slope Bernadette turned to the crowd and, with her arm outstretched, made an unmistakable sign to bow and kiss the ground.

Monsieur Estrade felt as though it concerned him alone. He had doubted, he had backslid, he had come close to denying his new-found faith. He thirsted for penance. He bowed and kissed the ground at his feet, without caring who saw it.

Behind him stood two servant girls of Lourdes

who had come with their mistresses. "She must be pretty conceited to think she can order people around like that", whispered one. And the other added, "All covered with mud as she is!"

Without looking back, Bernadette forcefully repeated her sign. And in the next instant no head remained unbowed, no knee unbent, no pair of lips untouched by the mud and slush of Massabieille. The first servant girl cried out and fainted away. Bernadette gave a start; she seemed about to faint herself, when Aunt Bernarde caught her and wiped the mud off her face, sighing, "If this is a trial, we must bear it."

As the crowd slowly broke up, the stone-cutter's daughter knelt down by the new spring. She had brought a bottle of holy water, in case the spring had disappeared, and now she emptied it on the ground of the grotto and filled it again at the spring. Then, careful not to spill a drop, she went away.

On her way home she saw Bernadette resting on a rock. Her godmother and some others hovered about, among them the schoolmistress. Bernadette had a coughing fit and was pressing her clasped hands to her chest.

"What happened today?" the schoolmistress wanted to know. "Did the Lady order all that? What did it mean?"

Bernadette struggled for breath. "The Lady said— 'Kiss the ground for sinners'", she gasped out and went on coughing.

The other girl hurried home.

"Did you get it?" her father called as soon as he heard her steps.

"Yes, Papa, I got it", she said, trying to keep her voice steady and her tears silent.

The stone-cutter's hands shook. He did not dare reach for the precious bottle. He knelt down and prayed and asked his daughter to pour the water into the hollow of his hand. Then he bathed his eyes in it with great reverence and prayed for a long time.

All of a sudden he shouted, "It's getting lighter!" He grabbed his daughter's arm and looked straight into her eyes, as he had not done in years. "You're crying", he said. "Why?"

The doctor did not like patients to speak before he spoke to them, but there were times when he had to put up with it. He could not well be harsh to the stone-cutter who came into the office, clutching his daughter's hand and stammering, "Doctor, I'm cured—I'm cured—"

Compassionately, the doctor shook his head. His sight is gone, he thought; now he's losing his mind!

"I'm cured", the man repeated. "I put some water from the grotto on my eyes, and now I see. I can see you and everything, Doctor."

The doctor cleaned his glasses. Bending over his desk until his nose nearly touched it, he wrote his opinion of the case on a piece of paper. "Can you read?" he asked, holding the paper under the patient's nose.

The stone-cutter did not need to look as closely as the doctor. "This man", he read aloud, "is suffering from in—incurable—a—mau—rosis." He looked proud of having stumbled so little over the difficult words.

The doctor sat as if a thunderbolt had struck at his feet. Was his own mind slipping? He sent the cured "incurable" home and decided to make a report on the case to the university, where greater scientists than he would know how to explain it. After all, miracles no longer happened in this day and age.

7

MESSAGES

S HE OUGHT TO STAY IN BED", Aunt Bernarde said
on Saturday, coming home from the grotto. The
family gathered around the mattress on which Bernadette sat, coughing from time to time. The spells
subsided slowly. Mother brought a pail of water and
started scrubbing Bernadette's muddy skirt. "Slob",
Toinette said disdainfully, and Father wondered how
soon the police would throw the lot of them in jail.

97

The police chief, at the same time, wondered when his gullible friends would stop boring him with tales of the daily vision. It was like sorcery; every time he considered the problem solved, something came along to make it knottier. This trickle of water, for instance. Of course, it made sensible people laugh: "First a lady out of thin air, now water from the rock—it's probably been raining into the grotto." But for each of these, there were ten ready to call it a miracle. The chief concluded that he had better wait for the rain to stop, the ground to dry out, and the new puddle to go away.

He looked for his wife and found her with Mademoiselle Estrade. "I'm so glad to see you", Mademoiselle cried and began to tell the chief about his lovable constable. The good man had been so moved today he could no longer contain himself, shouting, "Kiss the ground, all of you!" and setting the example then and there, over and over—

"I hope he cleaned his uniform", the chief said drily, excused himself, and went to his office to give the good man a piece of his mind.

But the constable had something on his own mind. "It's too much for that little girl", he glumly told his superior. "I can't even hear her breathing when she kneels on that stone. She's like a post planted there. She can't keep it up, sir."

I wouldn't have such luck, thought the chief. He said, "Let's have your report."

"Well," said the constable, "today the gendarmes had counted two thousand. They were like birds on the branches. The Blessed Virgin surely had a hand in the business—"

"You mind your business and leave the Virgin to the priests", snapped the police chief. "You mean to tell me there's no disorderly conduct?"

The constable said he never had any trouble. Folks mostly stayed on their knees as long as Bernadette did, and few dared to keep their hats on. "We behave as in church", he said simply.

The chief waved him out and drew up a brief report to his own superior, the Prefect of the Upper Pyrenees, at the provincial capital of Tarbes. He wrote: "Same scene, same exercises, more and more of the curious. . . ."

Two thousand, he thought uneasily. That was quite a crowd, even if they behaved as in church! The chief banged his fist on the table. Why in the name of all the saints didn't they pray in church, where they were supposed to?

The old parish church, in fact, was seeing more activity than ever, but also more confusion. Inquiries poured in on the Curé. Parishioners he had long seen only socially, such as the tax collector, suddenly came to confession. Regular communicants sought personal guidance. Night after night, the clip-clopping of wooden shoes under their windows kept them awake through the small hours of the morning, calling to the grotto as insistently as bells calling to church. What should they do?

On Sunday the Curé heard the confession of the servant girl who had fainted at Massabieille. She told him afterward that she had felt very much out of place. "I'm sorry I wasted my time, Father. In a church I feel I'm in the presence of God; down there I'm scandalized."

"All right, all right", said Father Peyramale. "There are some—and men among them, too—who have been impressed. Others are like you."

And he gave her his blessing and went off to think and to pray.

Monsieur Estrade, meanwhile, had gone to discuss the matter with the postmaster, who already knew all about it. "My daughters are crazy about the child", he said. "I don't know her, but I know her father. He's a poor devil who cleans my stables every Sunday. Hey, Soubirous!" he called.

Bernadette's father came out of the stable. "Monsieur?"

"My friend here has seen your daughter at the grotto", the postmaster said. "He thinks it was wonderful."

"Many people think so", said the father with a touch of pride.

"And what do you think?"

"I haven't seen it, Monsieur."

"What?" said the two gentlemen at once. "Unbelievable", the tax collector added as they went indoors.

François Soubirous finished his work and went home. In the alley he found Bernadette, in a white cape that he had never seen on her. Another girl was handing her a shiny rosary. "Please", she begged and ran off, leaving the beads in Bernadette's hand.

"A present?" Father asked sternly.

"Oh, no." She shook her head. "Pauline says it would make her happy if I used her rosary tomorrow, just once."

"And this?" He touched the new cape. It felt soft.

"It's Mademoiselle Estrade's", Bernadette said. "I'm to wear it to the grotto. The constable said he could clear the way more easily if I had on something white."

Her father looked after the girl who had left the rosary. "Pauline?" he wondered. "Don't her folks own the Virgin we use in the procession?" And when Bernadette nodded, he said nothing more.

In the morning, however, he went along for the first time. Bernadette walked between her mother and her godmother, and he followed right behind, ahead of some of the best people in town. He recognized the postmaster's daughters and the tax collector's sister. On the forest road there were eight or ten soldiers waiting. François Soubirous felt a pang of fear; but the leader only asked if Bernadette was the child who saw the Virgin. When someone said she was, he had his men form two lines and march ahead like an honor guard. The mass of people made Bernadette's father gasp. He had heard of it, of course, but had never really imagined that such crowds would come here on account of his daughter. When she knelt down, the soldiers took off their caps; the others bared their heads and sank to their knees, and all strained to see her, his child! It was the greatest moment in the life of François Soubirous.

Bernadette did not notice the actions of the people. She said her Our Fathers and her Hail Marys as she did every day, though the beads she moved were Pauline's. As on every day, a shudder of bliss seized her when the Lady appeared. But suddenly, faintly surprised, the Lady asked: "Where is your rosary?"

It was in Bernadette's pocket. She took it out and held it up, to show it to the Lady.

"Use that one", the Lady told her, with a smile.

At Bernadette's back a stir went through the thousands who could not see or hear. "She's having her rosary blessed", they whispered. "The Queen of Heaven must be blessing rosaries." And François Soubirous got up excitedly to cry out, "Quick! Rosaries in the air!"

A thousand rosaries were held up to the niche above the girl.

But Bernadette lovingly kissed the old, dark, shabby

one that was her own and had been preferred by the Lady.

Within an hour the incident was all over town. That shouldn't have happened, thought the chaplain. He called the child out of her catechism class to question her: "They tell me you blessed rosaries at the grotto this morning. Is that true?"

"Oh, no", she replied. "Women don't carry a stole to bless with."

"Did the Lady bless them? Everyone saw you raise yours toward the niche and copied you. What was the idea?"

Obediently Bernadette explained what had happened, and the chaplain took her explanation to the Curé, hoping to calm him. Father Peyramale was blazing. What outraged him above all was the role of the girl's father. "It's a wretched thing to have a family like that in town", he stormed. "They turn the place upside down—cause nothing but disorder."

"We might have reason to talk like this", the chaplain dared to say, "if we had examined the facts ourselves."

"We must not appear at the grotto", interrupted the Curé. "If we go, people will say we put her up to it. And if the thing comes to nothing, we'll be a laughingstock, and religion itself will suffer."

Bernadette's confessor followed him with his eyes about the room. If it came to nothing, he argued, would it not be better if the priests had looked into it and exposed the lie? Who else could give the Bishop the information he would need to pass judgment?

The Curé came to a dead stop. "I'll go and see the Bishop", he announced with vigor.

Three hours later, he drove his buggy through the streets of Tarbes into the courtyard of the Bishop's palace. He was received at once. In appearance, the Bishop of Tarbes was the very opposite of the Curé of Lourdes: almost seventy years old, slightly nervous, with a thin, lined face. There was a glint of amusement in his eyes as he regarded Father Peyramale. In Tarbes, he said, everyone was laughing at the so-called miracles of Lourdes.

Opinion in Lourdes was split, said the Curé, even among the clergy. His chaplain felt they might properly go to the grotto. "May we, my lord, or should we stand aloof?"

"If the dignity of religion permits, go", was the cautious answer.

"But, my lord," the Curé objected, "if we go, it will be said that we're behind this girl—that we encourage her to play these tricks."

The Bishop thought it over. "In that case," he decided, "don't go."

Thus Father Peyramale, back home, could tell his chaplain that the ban stood. No priest of Lourdes and surroundings must appear at the grotto. The little chaplain nodded humbly. Only three more days of the fortnight, he thought. Those, too, would pass.

Only three more days, Bernadette thought and could feel her heart breaking. How she would have loved on Tuesday to plead with the Lady to stay just a few moments longer! But the Lady only gave her a job to do and disappeared.

Bernadette knelt as though under a heavy burden. She could hardly get up. Clutching her godmother's arm, she stumbled through the disappointed crowd. The show had never been so short.

"I must take a message to Monsieur the Curé", Bernadette whispered.

Aunt Bernarde stiffened. She could still feel the shock of their last interview with the parish priest. "I won't go anywhere with you", she protested angrily. "You'll make us all ill. We're the ones who must put up with what people are saying."

Bernadette hesitated. "The Lady wants me to go to Monsieur the Curé", she said after a while.

"Oh, my goodness," wailed her aunt, "again!" But in the end she took her.

The Curé of Lourdes paced up and down his room when the innkeeper brought the child to him, after lunchtime. It was as if he did not even want to look at them. At last Bernadette spoke up: "The Lady wants a procession to the grotto, Father."

The priest stopped before the child. "You little

liar", he growled. "How dare you propose that we arrange a procession for your Lady?"

Bernadette backed up a step. "I didn't—"

"Hold her! Don't let her move!"

The little chaplain stepped out from the shadowy background to take Bernadette's arm. She stood still.

"I tell you, you see nothing", the Curé thundered. "A lady can't come out of a hole! You haven't told me her name—it *can't* be anything!" His eyes shot lightning. He was terrifying to watch. He told the girl she was going to be locked up and commanded her to find out the Lady's name.

"I ask her," Bernadette said, "but she starts laughing."

Now the Curé laughed—a hoarse, scornful laugh. "I'll tell you something. We'll do better than you ask. We'll give you a torch all for yourself, and you can run your own procession. People will follow you. *You* need no priests to follow you", he said witheringly.

"I don't ask anyone to come with me", Bernadette said in a small voice.

"You miserable child!" The priest resumed his pacing. "To think of it! A Lady! A procession!" He strode up and down the room once and halted again before Bernadette. She stood huddled in her cape, trembling a little, and never moved. Towering over her, he asked, "Are you quite sure the Lady asked for a procession on Thursday?"

Bernadette's mind was awhirl. On Thursday—that

was the last day, the farewell. A mist of tears made the priest's figure look hazy. If the procession did not take place Thursday, it would come too late. Just how had the Lady put it?

"Are you sure?" The Curé's voice was chilling.

The chaplain still held the girl's arm, more to keep her from falling than from running away. Her lips were white. She said nothing.

"Be careful, child", the chaplain gently warned her. "You must be certain of what you say. Did she want a procession on Thursday?"

With an effort, Bernadette whispered, "I think so—"

The Curé drew a breath of relief. "There", he snorted. "You're not even certain of it."

Bernadette wanted to answer, but no sound came from her lips. Father Peyramale strode to a corner and grabbed a broom that was leaning there. "Out!" he raged. "Get out—or I'll sweep you out with the broom!"

The chaplain dropped the girl's arm, and she ran out, her aunt behind her. They ran out of the house, across the yard, and into the street as if the broom were chasing them. The woman panted after the child but did not catch up until Bernadette stopped suddenly at a corner, clutching at her head. "Is anything wrong?" Aunt Bernarde asked, when she had regained her breath.

"What did I do," Bernadette moaned, "what did I

do! I forgot to give him half the message", she said in despair and turned around to go back.

"Oh, no, you don't." Her godmother took her by the neck and kept her firmly on the way to the Old Jail. "Once is enough", she said.

The broom was back in its place, in a corner of the Curé's room, but the Curé remained upset. With his arms folded behind him, he leaned over his chaplain. "Well? Do you still believe in her?"

The little chaplain did not answer directly. "It may take patience", he said. "When the drama is over, we can form a judgment."

Patience! Brats who saw visions certainly tried a man's patience, thought Father Peyramale. Just then someone knocked on the door. She wouldn't dare to come back—?

"Come in", he called.

His humor improved at once as the pretty young daughter of his old friend, the postmaster, appeared on the threshold. "Why, Dominiquette," he welcomed her, "what brings you here?"

She looked at him with the frankness that he liked about her. "The child who goes to the grotto wants to see you, Father."

Angry furrows rose on the brow of the parish priest. "I just threw her out", he said curtly.

Dominiquette nodded. "I know; I met her with her aunt. She says she didn't do as she was told."

"Hmm. I'm glad she realizes it."

"Her relatives refuse to bring her back", said the postmaster's daughter. "When may we come?"

We! The charming, dainty, sometimes a little haughty Dominiquette—with the lowliest child in town! The Curé was past surprise. "Bring her this evening at seven."

"Thank you, Father," cried the young lady and raised two pleading eyes to him, "but I beg you: don't frighten her so!"

"No, no, I won't."

"I'm only sorry you haven't seen her in ecstasy."

"I'm not", the Curé said coldly. "I'll see you at seven."

"Yes, Father. Good-bye." And Dominiquette was off to take the good news to the Old Jail.

In the evening, Lourdes was amazed to see the postmaster's daughter and the Soubirous girl walk arm in arm to the parish priest's door. "I wish the chaplain could be there again", Bernadette whispered to her new friend.

The chaplain was there again, and this time the Curé offered chairs to the two visitors. Bernadette refused hers. "I might dirty it", she said. Then, standing, she delivered the rest of her message: "The Lady in white whom I see at the grotto told me to tell the priests she wants a chapel at the grotto. She wants it at once, even if it's only a little one."

Now she knew that nothing had been forgotten. For an instant there was dead silence. Bernadette looked expectantly at the Curé, who stood before her like a statue.

"A chapel?" he repeated at last. "Is this like the procession, or are you sure?"

"Yes, Father. I'm certain."

He shrugged. "You say, 'the Lady in white'. Let me have her proper name."

"I keep asking, but she doesn't tell me", Bernadette said.

The priest bowed down to her. "Don't you see? She is having a game with you. Have you ever heard of fairies?"

"No, Father."

"Have you ever heard of witches?"

"No, Father."

"Father," Dominiquette broke in, "she can't understand you. Those are French words; in patois we have different words for fairies and witches. Bernadette knows only patois."

The Curé scowled; he did not like to use the local dialect. It was hard to deal with such a stubborn, ignorant child. Anyway, the Lady had to be answered. He drew himself up to his full height.

"The parish priest of Lourdes", he announced, "likes plain dealing. She wants a chapel and a procession? Tell your Lady to give us her name and a sign. Let her make the rosebush flower."

Another moment of silence; then the chaplain got up. "This is asking a miracle", he said.

The Curé turned to him. "Let her perform it, and we shall build her a chapel. It won't be a little one, either. It will be very big."

With that, he dismissed Bernadette and the postmaster's daughter. They felt deeply relieved, walking out through the garden of the parish church. Here, too, the roses were still lifeless and bare, but Bernadette happily squeezed the older girl's arm: "I'm so glad I've got this job done!"

8

THE PROCESSION

L OURDES WAS BUSTLING with curiosity. From the
postmaster's house, where Dominiquette told it
right after it happened, the story spread all over town.
Those who asked Bernadette heard her repeat obediently: "I must ask the Lady who she is and ask her to
make the rosebush bloom."

On Wednesday, Uncle André went along for the first time. The grotto was no longer a women's affair; was not Bernadette going there now on behalf of the Curé of Lourdes? The police had to clear a way for her party through the largest crowd the uncle had seen in his life—at least four thousand sightseers. They even flocked to the far bank of the river. The little girl kneeling on the flat stone before the dark niche was almost lost among the spectators. But above her, they saw what really tickled their curiosity that morning: the withered rosebush whose bloom, in winter, the parish priest had set as his price for a chapel.

The shabby old rosary ran through Bernadette's fingers. She prayed: "Hail Mary, full of grace . . ." But her thoughts ran ahead to matters she must not forget: the name—the rosebush—

The crowd waited. Most of them were on their knees, saying their beads. They no longer held them up for Bernadette to bless. There were some who snickered and wondered aloud how the Lady would meet the challenge. Those near Bernadette waited for the change in her appearance. It was slow in coming today. All one could see was the sad, plain face of a little peasant girl kneeling on the flat stone.

The crowd grew restless. Bernadette, deep in prayer, did not hear the impatient rumbles, but her uncle did. Those who had been out here all night were tired. A few quit and went home.

The uncle touched Bernadette's arm. She looked up; her eyes were dry and full of despair. "I won't see her any more", she whispered.

"There are too many people here", the uncle said and helped her to her feet. "Come home and have breakfast."

She hung her head and did as she was told. Mother looked fearfully about, moaning that now they would surely be put in prison. The crowd opened a path. It was like running a gauntlet of sneers and jibes.

"The Lady doesn't want to hear from the Curé", the jokers chuckled. "Wait till he gets to her followers!"

Mademoiselle Estrade went straight home, to avoid arguments. The postmaster's girls looked anxiously at their father, whom they had at last persuaded to come along; he had warned them not to expect him to be impressed by the sweet smiles of their little actress. Now he stood scowling after the grief-stricken child who disappeared on the forest road.

"If she's acting," the postmaster said at last, more to himself than to his daughters, "why didn't she just say she saw, like every other day?"

"Because she saw, every other day", they said, together.

"I believe it", said their father.

At the Old Jail, Uncle André took the Soubirous upstairs. He opened his cupboard, and soon the delicious smell of bacon and eggs filled the kitchen. The uncle set the dish before Bernadette, who sat with her head in her hands. She could not swallow a bite. "What did I do to her?" she mumbled brokenly. "Perhaps she's angry with me . . ."

The family watched her unhappily. Mother sighed; she couldn't stand this much longer. Rather than see the breakfast go to waste, the uncle ate it.

After an hour, Bernadette suddenly said she had to go to the grotto.

"No", Father barked. "You didn't see her this morning. That's all."

The girl's eyes sparkled. "Oh, I'll certainly see her now!"

"Won't you give it up?" Mother pleaded.

In the end, the uncle got up. "If you want to go back to the grotto," he told her, "we'll take the road by the fort and avoid the crowd."

They took the back road. The parents stayed home. It was nine o'clock when they came in sight of the grotto. Bernadette fell on her knees. From her lips came a breath of such happiness that it warmed the uncle's heart. He heard no more, although he saw the child's lips move. Was she giving the Lady the message? The morning's crowd had scattered. Only a few were still there; a few more came back in a hurry to see the uncle kneel beside his niece, awkwardly twisting his beret in his clasped hands. For he was not accustomed to prayer.

Eventually Bernadette turned to him. "The Lady was waiting", she said and rose from her knees.

He got up, too, and contentedly put on his beret again. Had he not told her they should take the back road?

"She was waiting", the child repeated, radiant with wonder. "She was waiting for me!"

On the way back, he asked if she had delivered the Curé's message.

She nodded. "I must bring him her answer."

"Without me", said Uncle André with a grin. She did not seem to mind. She went home to find her parents gone and no one around to ask questions. In the afternoon, she told her sister that she was going out to see the Curé.

"Look out for his broom", Toinette giggled.

Bernadette was no longer afraid of Father Peyramale. He, too, seemed to have been waiting. "What do you have to tell me today?" he demanded.

"The Lady smiled when I said you wanted her to make the rosebush bloom", the child replied. "She said she wants the chapel."

The veins bulged on the Curé's forehead, but he controlled himself. "Do you have money to pay for it?"

"No, Father", she said regretfully.

His voice rose. "Neither have I. Ask your Lady to give you some."

Bernadette left. From across the street, Dominiquette

saw her. She ran out to ask her little friend into the house, and they no sooner entered than the postmaster burst in so hastily that he forgot to leave his whip outside. "Did you see her?" he asked Bernadette.

"Yes, Monsieur." She smiled at him. "Will you come with me tomorrow?"

"I promise", said the postmaster.

Then Father came to take her back to the Old Jail. Her cousin Jeanne-Marie had arrived from the country. Bernadette hurried home; she was very fond of her cousin. They embraced, and Jeanne-Marie said she would like to spend the night in Lourdes and come out to the grotto in the morning.

Mother brought what little food there was left. "Eat now; talk later", she told the two girls, who went right on talking.

"I hear you didn't see the Lady today", Jeanne-Marie said worriedly. "Maybe you won't see her tomorrow, either?"

"I didn't see her this morning, but I did later in the day."

"Did she come to get you?"

Bernadette burst out laughing. "No, I just felt I had to see her. And when I got there, she was waiting for me!" Her eyes shone.

"Sit down and eat, you two", Mother broke in again. "We've arranged for you to sleep together, upstairs. You can chatter all night."

"They say people stay at the grotto all night to get

a good place", said the girl from the country. "How will I ever get near you?"

Bernadette thought for a moment. "Don't worry. You'll be there."

The most worried people in town were the officials: the police chief, the mayor, the gendarmes. What annoyed them especially was a new rumor that the Lady had not come on Wednesday because she was preparing the miracle for the Curé.

"As far as I'm concerned, it'll be miracle enough if we have no serious accidents", growled the police chief. Around the grotto people would be crushed on top of each other; with the rock above covered with sightseers, a single loose stone could result in disaster. It was all quite irregular, the chief thought, and he suggested to his superiors that Bernadette be medically examined.

The mayor, on his part, wrote a note to the commander of the military garrison. "The presence of large numbers of strangers threatened for tomorrow", he wrote, "obliges me to ask you to put your troops at my disposal in the interest of public order. Please have all available men at the town hall by six A.M." Then he put the note in his pocket and went to see the Curé.

"If the weather stays like this," he began and looked unhappily at the cloudless sky, "we expect to have fifteen or twenty thousand people here tomorrow, most of them out of curiosity about your miracle."

It was not his miracle, Father Peyramale responded coldly.

Of course not, the mayor hastily agreed. He brought out his request to the garrison commander. Would the Curé care to comment on it?

The priest read and nodded. Anything to ward off trouble was all right with him, he said, and the mayor left somewhat happier.

The lieutenant commanding the gendarmes of the district came to Lourdes to study the lay of the land around the grotto. He made a sketch, took some notes, and went to town to look at the area around Bernadette's house. The road was far from clean, but he saw five or six people kneeling there in fervent prayer. "If there are many like that about tomorrow," he muttered, amazed, "my men will be worn out."

At the Citadel he gave final orders to the sergeant: "Don't show yourself too obviously. Instruct your men to keep side arms in their pockets. Field uniform, as for military duty."

"Yes, sir", said the sergeant.

"Set up one-way traffic on the road to the grotto. Have those going keep to the left; those returning, to the right."

"Yes, sir", said the sergeant.

"As for miracles, leave them to the civil officials. Miracles are their business; ours is to keep order and control traffic—nothing else. Go to it."

"Yes, sir", the sergeant said once more, and the lieutenant rode off.

None of the officials went to bed that night. At 11 P.M. the police chief went to Massabieille for a rigorous search of the grotto. If preparations had been made for a "miracle", he was going to find them. The gendarme sergeant was there, too, for the same purpose. They inspected the spring, which the chief had never seen and never quite believed in; some of the townsmen had built a small basin of bark for it, and it seemed to yield about a quart of water every second.

The chief had to admit that the spring was a fact. He and the sergeant jointly went over every piece of rock in the cave and found five copper coins, a broken rosary, and a nosegay of rosebuds and laurel leaves.

At 4 A.M. they returned and had a hard time getting through. People then stood too tightly packed to move a limb, but no one was heard complaining. With difficulty, the officials fenced off a small space, so there would later be room for themselves and Bernadette and her relatives.

By half-past six, the crowd was overflowing on all sides. The sawmill meadow across the canal was packed, and thousands lined the far bank of the river. The chief looked up from the grotto and saw a whole mob hanging on the rock; if one fell, he was sure to drag ten others with him. The gendarmes had all their men from Lourdes and nearby towns on hand, besides the detachment of soldiers. They were posted between the town and the grotto, and their sergeant was everywhere at once, asking people to keep calm. But, thought the chief, a dam was a feeble thing to hold back tide of this kind, even if it was a dam of policemen!

The chief hoped that the girl would come as usual, before seven o'clock, but she was late. The distant bells of Lourdes tolled the seventh hour, and still there was no Bernadette. Would she fail to show up, as her Lady had done yesterday? The chief shuddered to think of it. The crowd was losing patience. He heard angry murmurs. He drew his big gold watch and stared at the dial, as if that might help. The minutes crawled.

By 7:15 the police chief was wishing as hard that the girl would come to the grotto as he had been wishing for weeks that she would stay away.

Bernadette could not come on time because she was being looked over by three gentlemen. They were city doctors whom the Prefect had sent, on the police chief's suggestion, to examine her. For two hours they bothered her with questions, knocking on her chest and listening on her back, and failed to find anything wrong with her that enough food wouldn't cure. She did not even cough once. Only as the clock struck seven from the parish church, she winced a little.

"I must get ready now", she said politely.

Cousin Jeanne-Marie, aquiver with impatience, was relieved to see the doctors allow Bernadette to dress. They turned to her mother, and one of them said, "If you stay much longer in this damp hole, you'll all get sick." Then they left the Old Jail.

Father, Uncle André, Aunt Bernarde with her blessed candle, the constable, the postmaster, and many, many more were waiting outside to escort Bernadette to the grotto. Mother stayed home today with the other children. She was afraid of the crowd—and tomorrow, God willing, it would be all over, anyway. The two girls ran out together.

They took the back road under the Citadel, but that, too, was so full of people that Jeanne-Marie clung to her cousin's arm for fear of being separated. "Don't worry, you'll be near me", Bernadette assured her. It was all she said on the long way through the thickening crowds.

On the forest road, the police managed to clear the way for Bernadette and her group; but they did not know Jeanne-Marie, so the crowd kept closing in again in front of her. On the path to the grotto, she lost sight of her cousin. She was far behind, wedged in so tightly that all she could see was the sky. She had almost given up hope, when suddenly a voice shouted: "Bernadette is asking for one of her cousins!"

"Here I am," she cried as loudly as she could, "but I can't move!"

From below, two uniformed men elbowed their way through to her, took her by the hands, and led her down. The taller one wore a broad official sash. "Is this the one you want?" he asked Bernadette, who stood in an enclosure guarded by two gendarmes.

"Yes", she said. The tall man nodded to the gendarmes. "All right, Chief", they said and passed Jeanne-Marie through the barrier.

An indescribable sense of joy and happiness overcame the young girl as she knelt and prayed with Bernadette.

All around them, men bared their heads, and men and women, near and far, sank to their knees.

In the distant parish church of Lourdes, the Curé knelt before the altar of Mary Immaculately Conceived. "If thou art she whom the child sees at the grotto," he prayed, "if it is in thy name that she asks for a procession and a chapel—grant me a sign!"

The little chaplain had left the church by the side entrance and followed the row of dry rosebushes into the square. The usually so-crowded place was empty; Lourdes was like a town whose inhabitants had fled in panic. Everywhere there was the same silence, the same solitude. Everyone was at the grotto.

The chaplain, under orders to keep away, yielded to an irresistible desire and walked on—not to Massabieille, but along the other side of the river. Finally, he found a chestnut grove on a slope. From there, the rock was hidden only by a wooded hill. The sky was clear, the sun just beginning to gild the mountains and the valley. The early morning stillness was broken only by the faint, confused murmur of the crowd that barely reached his ear. Now, it ran through his mind, now she must be seeing! And he deeply regretted that he was not free to watch the scene.

Across the river, the police chief was on his knees, four steps from Bernadette. He knelt because everyone did, but he had his notebook out to record her moves and count her smiles. He looked at his watch; her abnormal state had now lasted half an hour. From indications described to him, it must be near its end.

The crowd was quiet, hardly stirring. Soldiers and gendarmes stood ready to direct it back to town in good order, according to plan. The rosebush under the niche was unchanged, dry and bare, as the girl's features began to resume their ordinary peasant appearance. The chief was pleased. There had been no miracle. In a short while, everything would be over.

The priest in the grove had his rosary in his hands and his eyes cast down before him. In his ear was the hum of the thousands, swelling and fading and swelling again, until it seemed to soar on a tide of angels' voices. He looked up. He could not see the grotto because of the hill in front of him, but he saw the crowds in the meadow and along the forest road. He saw them move and line up to form an endless, orderly train that slowly circled Massabieille and moved back to town, chanting sacred hymns.

The little chaplain made the Sign of the Cross. In the glory of the rising sun, a human sea—a sprawling torrent of people—was transformed before his eyes into a solemn procession.

9

"I AM—"

Bernadette's eyes clung to the rosebush where the golden roses on the bare feet of the Lady had vanished, leaving only the thorns. She thought she could still see a glow in the darkening niche. But the people around her thought they could see a golden glow on Bernadette's dark hair as she slowly came back to earth.

Leaning on her cousin's arm and followed by the family and a few neighbors, she went home through the woods. On the bridge she halted a moment, to look back, and had to smile at the sight of the many people singing pious songs and moving in such good order around Massabieille and back. She had not been wrong, after all: it was on this Thursday that the Lady had wanted her procession.

"You smiled the same way at the grotto", her cousin said. "Why?"

"I smile because the Lady smiles", said Bernadette.

"And why did you move your lips as though you were talking?"

Bernadette laughed. "I was talking out loud, just as I'm talking now. The Lady spoke, too."

And Jeanne-Marie, who had not heard a thing, fell into puzzled silence.

They no sooner reached the Old Jail than a huge crowd filled the alley. A few, mostly women, got into the house before the door could be bolted. The uncle sent Bernadette upstairs, but they came after her, to kiss and embrace her or at least to touch her hand. "Why do you touch me?" she asked, bewildered. "I have no power."

They begged her to touch their rosaries. "What do you want me to do with them? I'm not a priest", she said, annoyed. She turned away—and saw Jeanne-Marie standing like the rest, holding out three rosaries. "What?" she cried, "you, too?"

The family came up, and more strangers. Uncle André tried to get the first group out the back way, but they would not leave unless Bernadette touched their rosaries. "Oh, all right", she said at last. "Give them to me; I'll put them with mine." She turned them over and over with her own and gave them back. She said, "Keep them—not because I've touched them, but because they've touched the one I use at the grotto."

"Bernadette!" voices rose from the alley. "Bernadette!"

She went to the window. Before the house, a line of gendarmes was trying to hold back the crowd. Only those who had rosaries were let through; at the door, two husky neighbors helped Uncle André to keep them moving. "Bernadette!" cried a hundred voices. "Bless us! Bless us!"

Shocked, she withdrew from the window.

Watching the scene from the corner of the alley were the police chief and the gendarme sergeant. "It's odd", the chief said, shaking his head. "There was no miracle; they should have been disappointed. And now they're storming her house!"

"I heard of it just in time", said the sergeant, pleased with himself. "It was a bad situation. When the ignorant get religion, their love of relics outweighs their respect for property. If we hadn't stepped in, that poor house might end up in the pilgrims' pockets."

What interested the chief was not so much what

the pilgrims took out of the house as what they took in. He had heard that the girl's parents were charging a fee to those who wished to see her.

"We'll find out", the sergeant said. He gave an order to a gendarme.

Upstairs people kept filing in and out endlessly. They touched Bernadette's hand, and the bolder women kissed and hugged her with all their hearts. In the alley, her name was shouted until she came to the window again, and again.

"Did you give anyone any money?" the gendarme asked all those leaving the house. They all said they had not. Most of them had tried to give her something and met with a firm, if polite, refusal. One man said, "I know your parents are poor; take it for them!" and she answered, "My parents can work." So many people crowded into the small room that once, when a copper coin fell to the ground, it could not be found until Bernadette saw her little brother stoop and slip something into his pocket.

"Jean! You thief!" She flew at him and slapped his face. He returned the coin, in tears.

It went on for hours. Finally, only one foreign lady remained. She begged the girl to take money or gifts or to let her have her rosary in exchange for money— all in vain. In the end, she offered a few oranges. "Well, yes, Madame," Bernadette said, "if you'll stay and eat them with us."

The lady gladly agreed. And Bernadette took her

own orange slice and gave it to Jean, to make up for the slap in the face.

At last the lady left, too. It was evening. The crowd had scattered; the family had gone downstairs. Only Jeanne-Marie stayed with her cousin. Then the door opened once more, gently, and Dominiquette's pretty head appeared. She just wanted to look after Bernadette for a moment. "Aren't you very tired?"

"Oh, yes," Bernadette sighed, "I'm tired of all that kissing!"

But she still had a job to do. She had to report to the Curé. Jeanne-Marie and Dominiquette went along but waited outside. The parish priest already knew everything from the chaplain and from the police; he mentioned neither the rosebush nor the procession. He just wanted to know what the Lady had said this time.

"I asked for her name, but she only smiled again", Bernadette said.

His face darkened. "Until she tells you her name, I can't do what she asks", he decided. "You'll have to ask her again." Then his voice mellowed. "If she is the Blessed Virgin, of course, I'll do whatever she wants."

Bernadette thought she was dismissed. She turned to go, but the priest called her back and bent down to her. "Did she tell you to come back?"

"No, Father."

"Did she say she wouldn't come back herself?"

"No, she didn't say that", Bernadette answered, quickly but with proper restraint and humility, though all her hopes lay in that single sentence.

The chief of police had every right to hope that this nerve-wracking Thursday, March 4, might end the nasty business. He could point with pride to the performance of his duties and to the miracle he had accomplished in avoiding even the slightest accident. That the Lady had failed to perform her own expected miracle had pleased him further. A third point in his favor was the spell of bad weather that now set in. It was weather you wouldn't have turned out a dog in; it was bound to affect the sensation-hunters at Massabieille. The chief felt he was doing all right. He kept a careful eye on the Old Jail and was glad to hear that visitors who wished to see the girl found the door shut nowadays. Another week, he thought, and people will be sick of it all.

He was mistaken. The people of Lourdes were only sick at the idea that it might all be over. They could not bear to think that there should really be no more wonderful events. All sorts of rumors started: a lame boy was said to be able to walk, a blind girl to see, a deaf woman to hear. The doctor, to be sure, could tell at a glance that these patients walked, saw, and heard only as well as before, but the rumors continued. The story that a halo had been seen around Bernadette's head was even mentioned—mockingly, of course, in the newspapers of Tarbes. And her stubborn refusal to accept money or gifts in the Lady's behalf was actually resented.

In the end, the cobbler's wife had an idea. If the presents were given to the Lady herself, perhaps she would come again? The baker's wife promptly agreed. They decided to start with a modest sanctuary lamp, for which they could raise the small sum needed in their own circle of friends. A day or two later, they carefully hung the lamp by a wire from the ceiling of the grotto. To make sure that it would never go out—no more than the sanctuary lamp in church—they put a bottle of oil and some wicks on the ground underneath, so that anyone who saw it burning low might refill it.

There was a continual coming and going at the grotto. The police found the water from the spring unfit to drink, but the people thought differently. No one could tell how much of it had, in fact, been drunk or otherwise used against every kind of ailment. And whenever they drank, washed, prayed, or lighted candles in the cave, the devout would drop a few coins into the alms-box, a little basket that had been put up at the entrance, protected by a wooden grille.

"I regret having to bore you once more with this affair", the chief of police wrote to the Prefect on March 19. Bernadette had not entered the grotto since the fourth, but the chief admitted that, for five days now, the believers' zeal had been more obvious than ever. For example, last Sunday two lighted candles had been put up at the rear of the cave. On Monday there had been three; on Tuesday, five; on Wednesday, ten—also a bone crucifix on the inner wall, decorated with laurel and boxwood. What next? the chief asked himself.

As though in reply, his faithful constable reported that a board to hold a quantity of candles was being made in town, because people had trouble getting them to stand up on the ground. The board would be ready well in advance of the Easter festivities, said the constable.

"Well," said the chief, "won't that be a joyous Easter!" The children, too, played a part—encouraged, perhaps, by the example of the schoolmistress who had once kept Bernadette away from the grotto. She now brought two offerings of her own: an image of the Sacred Heart and a picture, "Madonna of the Birds." After that, no parents in Lourdes could deny their children something to take to Massabieille. The most successful in this drive was Pauline; she persuaded her family to present Bernadette's Lady with their statue of the Virgin that was used in the procession each year.

On Tuesday before the feast of the Annunciation, at eight o'clock in the evening, the statue was solemnly installed in the grotto, in the festive gleam of candlelight shining on miraculous medals, crowns, rosaries, carvings, banners, and framed holy pictures.

The little plaster Virgin stood in a wire shell covered with moss and flowers; it was not much of an "ornamental shrine", as the police chief described it, but it was beloved in Lourdes. There were at least six hundred people present, and every child envied Pauline, who had the honor of assisting at the presentation.

Among those who had come to see Pauline's great moment was the girl whose jealous rage had once caused the rockslide at the grotto. It was Jeanne's first visit to Massabieille since the affair that was still heavy on her conscience. In her pocket was the money she had earned in five weeks of rag-picking: ten copper coins. If she put those into the box for the Lady, Jeanne thought, her evil prank would be forgiven— especially as she had heard that this morning, when the money was counted, there had been thirty-one silver francs and ninety centimes. Her ten coppers would make it an even thirty-two francs.

After the little statue was installed, there was a sudden uproar. "Out of the way!" people cried. "Make way for the poor man who has seen the Blessed Virgin!"

On the stone where Bernadette used to kneel, there squatted a beggar who waved one of his crutches and repeated to himself like a crazy man: "I saw her—I saw her—she was just here—I saw her—"

He was led away by the constable and a gendarme. Most of the people followed the new sensation: only a few grown-ups stayed with Pauline and Jeanne in the glittering grotto. All at once Jeanne cried out: "The money—it's gone! Police—it was thirty-one ninety—police!" But all the policemen had gone off with the beggar.

Next morning, as Bernadette came from her catechism class, walking beside a sister, a hairy hand gripped her arm. It belonged to the man who repaired the roads in town and also served as deputy to the police chief.

"What do you want of me?" Bernadette asked.

"Come along", said the road mender gruffly.

The sister had tears in her eyes. "You're going to kill this child", she protested. "I beg you, leave her to us!"

Bernadette laughed at the road mender. "Hold me tight, or I'll run away", she warned him.

She was taken before the police chief, who looked grim and gleeful at the same time. "Now I've got you, you and your fine family", he barked at the child. "When I find the money that has been collected at your grotto, you'll all go to prison. I'll have your home searched at once."

"You'll find no money there", Bernadette said.

"You can stay in jail till I do", snapped the chief.

"I'm ready", she said gaily. "But if your jail isn't stronger than the one we live in, I'll get out."

"We'll see about that. Constable!" he shouted. "Where in the name of all the saints is that constable?"

A moment later the constable rushed in. "You want me, Chief? I just went to the church, to give Monsieur the Curé the money from the grotto", he apologized. "It was almost thirty-two francs. I thought it wouldn't be safe out there."

The chief stared at him and at the girl.

Bernadette said nothing, but she became very serious. What was it the Curé had said to her? "Do you have money? Ask your Lady to give you some." Since then, the police had first arranged the procession— and now they had brought the parish priest some of the Lady's money!

"You go home and behave", the chief grunted and made up his mind to go and see for himself what was going on at Massabieille.

When he got there, he could hardly believe his eyes. "The grotto has been transformed into a regular chapel", he reported to the Prefect that evening. He had to bore him again, indeed.

Our Lady's Day, March 25, was on Thursday that year.

During the night before, Bernadette awoke to a call. The voice that she had once said she could hear in her heart was calling. For a moment her heart stood still. Then it beat faster and faster, and Bernadette got up to rouse her parents, without whose consent she could not go. At first they bluntly refused. It was past four o'clock by the time they gave in. They both came along as she set out on the familiar road; on the

way they picked up Aunt Bernarde and Dominiquette
and the baker's wife—perhaps a half-dozen close
friends. Another dozen or so were already at Massabieille at that uncommonly early hour. Fewer than
twenty people, all told, surrounded the child as she
knelt again on the familiar stone, sliding her old rosary
through her fingers.

For the first time Bernadette saw the cave lighted
by the lamp and all the candles, with the crucifix, the
holy pictures around, and the statue in the little wire
shell. But the golden glow that filled the grotto came
not from the candles.

The Lady looked about her, fondly gazing on the
little statue in the shell. Her blue eyes shone, the blue
sash molded her white gown, the golden roses gleamed
on her bare feet as she came closer. Perhaps she was
really taller than Bernadette. Or did it only seem that
way because the child was kneeling?

Bernadette knelt without stirring, fearful of brush-
ing against the cross that hung from the luminous
rosary, golden as the roses on the Lady's feet. She
dared not move because the Lady was so close—
closer than ever before. Her hands were held out to
the child.

Bernadette bowed very low. She summoned her
courage to ask: "Please, Mademoiselle, would you tell
me who you are?"

The Lady smiled.

Bernadette asked again: "Please, Mademoiselle,

would you have the great kindness to tell me who you are?"

The Lady smiled.

Bernadette asked again: "Please, Mademoiselle— though I am unworthy."

The Lady raised her hands and joined them over her breast. She raised her eyes from Bernadette to heaven. "I am"—she spoke as if it were a confession, not a revelation—"I am the Immaculate Conception."

Humbly Bernadette listened to the words that she could hear only in her heart, while the smiling image vanished.

Bernadette rose from her knees. She put her cheap little candle into the grotto with the rest. The golden glow was gone. Only the candles flickered.

Bernadette was unable to speak. In her mind, lest she forget it, she kept memorizing the sentence the Lady had entrusted to her. First she would have to tell it to her confessor, she thought, repeating the difficult syllables every step of the way.

She gave the message to the chaplain quite naturally, in the patois of Lourdes, just as she had received it. He nodded and took her hand. "Come", he said. "Tell the name to Monsieur the Curé."

The Curé was in the sacristy, preparing for morning Mass. "Well?" he asked as usual. "What do you have to tell me today?"

Bernadette answered eagerly. "I asked her who she is, and she said, 'I am the Immaculate Conception.'"

The Curé took a step backward, as though doubting his ears. "What does that mean?" he asked.

"I don't know", replied the child. "That's why I repeated it to myself all the way up."

The parish priest took her by the hand and led her into the church, to the altar that carried the image with the words MARY IMMACULATELY CONCEIVED. His finger pointed at the golden letters.

The chaplain had followed them. "The child can't read", he reminded his superior in a low voice.

So the Curé read the legend aloud, word after word, and explained, "It means 'conceived without sin'. By a gift of God, our Lady has always been free from original sin. Perhaps she was just mentioning her immaculate conception?"

"No, Father", Bernadette said. "She told me who she is."

"Think carefully", the priest warned her. "Once before, you could not remember her exact words. How can the joyful Virgin Mary have said that she *is* 'the immaculate conception'?"

Bernadette did not have to think. She repeated, "I heard her say it."

The Curé did not give up. "It is one of her qualities," he explained, "but it cannot be your Lady's name."

Bernadette joined her hands before the picture of the Virgin: "Our Lady in the grotto said, 'I am'."

10

AT THE CROSSROADS

NIGHT AND DAY the candles burned for our Lady in the grotto. People brought her crosses and hearts, rings and bracelets, earrings and chains. There were now three statues of the Virgin in the cave, all covered from head to toe with the gifts of the faithful. No one came empty-handed. A paralyzed tailor from Tarbes threw the first gold piece among the offerings, and a poor old peasant woman brought a cheese and cried, "It's for the Blessed Virgin!"

The tinsmith made a basin of zinc with three pipes to catch the spring. The quarry men blasted a wider path out of the rock and built a rail for the chapel. They did it evenings, after their days of hard work. The blind, the lame, and the incurably ill came in droves from near and far, in carriages or on foot.

The police chief was at his wit's end. A note of despair crept into his reports to the Prefect: "I daresay, Monsieur, that if this business is left to itself, it will never stop . . ."

The Prefect was no longer bored; he was furious. He reminded the chief that any new place of worship must be authorized by both the Church and the state. This whole grotto was against the law, and the police had to enforce the law. It might be well to impress this on the local clergy, the Prefect added.

The chief hastened to see the Curé. But the Curé would not commit himself. The priests of Lourdes had carefully avoided the grotto. They had nothing to do with it. If someone else had broken the law— why, Father Peyramale had full confidence in the police. Now, if the chief would excuse him, he had problems of his own to discuss with his chaplain.

The Curé was not worrying about the authority for a new altar in his parish; what worried him was the authority for Bernadette's last message. Was it indeed our Lady who had appeared to the child? He could not be sure. He had prayed for a sign, and the girl had brought him a name that did not sound like one. To his knowledge, no one but Bernadette Soubirous had ever referred to the Blessed Mother of

God as "The Immaculate Conception". Father Peyramale shook his head. "Her expression cannot be correct."

"Whose?" asked the chaplain. "The child's or the Lady's?"

The Curé did not answer but sat down to write the Bishop. He related the facts of his last talk with the child, without comment. He stressed that he had given her no support whatever. He humbly submitted that the Church should perhaps investigate and decide now, before some action by the civil power prevented it. And he asked for orders.

The Bishop had just read this letter when a footman announced the Prefect of the Upper Pyrenees. The great man strode in, made a gesture of kissing the Bishop's ring, and demanded that the Church make up its mind and speak out, one way or the other. If the visions at Lourdes were genuine, he said, they should be approved; if they were false, they ought to be condemned.

The Bishop of Tarbes listened calmly to the outraged master of the province. "I do not share your view", he said then. "A bishop's duty in these difficult circumstances is to refrain from personal judgment and to wait till Providence reveals the truth."

The Prefect argued, coaxed, and threatened, but the Bishop stood firm. Afterward, he gave the same answer to the Curé of Lourdes.

"I have my duty to do; I cannot shirk it", the

Prefect declared. The Soubirous girl was at the root of the trouble; the thing to do was to remove her from the scene. How? On what grounds? The Prefect asked the officials of Lourdes. They ought to know. Unfortunately, they didn't.

The gendarme sergeant, despite a close watch, had found nothing to show that Bernadette or her family had profited by her fame. Fistfuls of gold had been pressed on her and refused. Had her father taken half of what he was offered daily, he would not be the poorest but one of the richest men in Lourdes now, said the gendarme.

The police chief remained suspicious. But he admitted that he had no proof, either. He thought Bernadette should be locked up, because if she were not a cheat, she must be crazy.

The Imperial prosecutor, whose job it was to bring criminals to justice, doubted whether locking her up would help. He felt the pot was kept boiling by people who hoped to make money out of the pilgrims.

The mayor's reaction was the most surprising. He rather liked to see his sleepy town so full of strangers. They were good for business. What attracted them was the spring, to which the miracle rumors gave so much free publicity. So the mayor proposed examining the water, rather than Bernadette, to find out what it was good for, and to make Lourdes a health resort.

After all this advice, the Prefect decided to let Bernadette make just one more false step.

One for whose business the grotto was good was the doctor. He had to see more patients, not fewer; for almost all those who hoped to be cured by a miracle wanted to hear his opinion, too. Of course, he found most of them improved only in their imagination— or in their faith, if you would like to put it that way.

On Tuesday after Easter, a fifteen-year-old peasant boy showed up at the doctor's in a pitiful state. When he stripped, his chest was one great sore. The doctor knew at once that this poor fellow was on his way to the grotto, but he felt it his duty to warn him. "Don't let cold water get anywhere near that ulcer; it's the very thing to make it worse", he cautioned the sick boy and gave him an ointment.

"Thank you", said the patient. "Good-bye."

The doctor shook his head. That boy was going to bathe his sores at the spring, first thing tomorrow. They all did. They all hoped for a miracle. Well, there had really been no explanation for the stone-cutter's cure, but that did not make it a miracle. There were many things left in nature that science could only observe and not yet explain.

The doctor felt a sudden pang of curiosity. He had been at the grotto before, without observing anything miraculous; Bernadette believed in her hallucinations, that was all. But how would it be to go out tomorrow

and see whether the boy with the ulcer was there—
and, if so, how he reacted to the icy water?

It was Wednesday, the seventh of April. Daybreak
now came so early that the doctor left his lantern at
home. At the grotto he was hailed all around. The
stone-cutter and his daughter waved, and the postmaster's Dominiquette taunted him cheerily: "Spying
on the competition?" The ground around the carefully channeled spring looked indeed like an outdoor
hospital. The morning dew had misted the doctor's

glasses; he wiped them to look among his many
patients for the boy of yesterday, when the crowd
suddenly stirred. There was the same excited muttering as on that other Wednesday when the doctor
had been here first. "Here she come—here she
comes—"

It was Bernadette, with her parents and her god-mother carrying a blessed candle, just as six weeks before.

The doctor managed to get through to Bernadette and to stay by her side when she lit the candle and knelt down. The whole crowd knelt with her. The doctor stooped low, to be able to see her better, but she did not notice him. She immediately fell into a trance. Her rosary hung from her left hand; in her right she held the lighted candle. She smiled and bowed. Then she got up to enter the grotto, with her left hand shielding the flame of the candle in her right. Her fingers were spread apart; the doctor saw the flame licking between them. A gust of wind bent it directly against her hand.

"She's burning herself", cried a few women nearby, but the doctor held them back. He wanted to see what would happen. The flame seemed to have no effect on Bernadette. On the contrary, she kept cradling it closely in her left hand—the hand that held the rosary.

The doctor peered at his watch, again and again. For fifteen minutes he observed her in this position. How could that be? Was her skin insensitive to fire? He wiped his glasses and held his watch to his ear. It was ticking normally. When he looked again, Bernadette was getting up to leave.

He stopped her. "Will you show me your left hand, please?"

She readily held it out. The doctor examined the palm and all fingers and found no trace of a burn. Then he asked for her candle, lighted it quickly, and brought it close to the puzzling hand.

"You're burning me", cried Bernadette and snatched the hand away.

The doctor was too stunned to say he was sorry. He could not doubt what he had seen with his own eyes. For fifteen minutes, he had seen Bernadette's hand unharmed by fire. That was a miracle.

A miracle, he kept repeating to himself on the way home, a miracle. He had completely forgotten why he had come. At his office he found his young patient of yesterday. "What happened?" asked the doctor.

"I went to the grotto last night", said the boy. "I couldn't wait. I bathed my chest at the spring, and then I took some of the water with me and went on praying and washing my sores all night. Then I fell asleep and awoke after seven—like this." He bared his chest.

The ulcer had disappeared. In its place was firm, white scar tissue.

The doctor nodded, as if he had expected nothing else. "Pray, my boy", he said. "Bernadette works miracles."

"What our doctor says about the affair is not to be taken seriously any more", the police chief noted in his report to the Prefect about "the so-called miracle of the candle".

So she did it again, thought the Prefect. This went too far—and he promptly sent for three other doctors who were supposed to examine the girl once more and find her insane.

The police chief also sent for Bernadette again. "The doctor says you work miracles", he began.

She laughed. "The doctor is fibbing."

"I'm glad you know that", the chief said grimly. "Then I suppose you know, too, that you're not going to the grotto any more."

He expected a protest, but she simply nodded. "I know", she said without surprise.

The chief was speechless. He just waved her away.

Bernadette stayed away from the grotto, but the crowds kept coming. One heard of more and more people who arrived at the spring on stretchers or crutches, feeling their way with canes or writhing in pain, and walked away unaided. The doctor still doubted many of these cures and knew how to explain others, but some baffled him.

Then—about a week after Bernadette's last visit, as if it should be quite clear that she had nothing to do with it—others started seeing things at Massabieille. First they were only children "playing vision", but soon grown women climbed all over the grotto and niche and told wondrous tales.

The mayor appointed an investigating committee. Among the members were the town clerk, the road mender, and the constable. The committee traced every step of the new "seers". It climbed where they had climbed, knelt where they had knelt, put candles where they had put candles. It found nothing supernatural, but it found out all about the grotto. The famous cave was formed by a huge, overhanging rock ledge sloping inward and downward to a round cell. From an opening in the ceiling, eight feet above the ground, a passage led up to the niche. It took a ladder to reach the passage. To get to the niche you had to squeeze into the opening, as a lizard squeezes into a crack, and to crawl flat on your stomach for fifteen feet.

"Into this passage", the mayor reported to the Prefect, "have gone not only men but women and girls. Modesty should indeed have kept them out of a spot where they would be forced to bend and twist in such a manner!"

The grotto report reached the Prefect, together with the new doctors' report on Bernadette. They had examined her at length, at the hospice. They agreed that she ate, drank, and slept marvelously. She had coughing spells, but no signs of other ailments. In fact, the doctors found her healthy in body and mind; but as they could not admit that her story might be true, they concluded: "She may have been the victim of a hallucination."

For the Prefect that was enough.

Spring had come to the Pyrenees. The shepherds moved their flocks out on the mountain slopes; the birds twittered in the fresh green of trees and shrubs; hawthorn and boxwood scented the road to Massabieille, where Bernadette had not been seen for weeks; and the Prefect called on thirty-seven mayors and other high officials of the province to meet him in Lourdes.

When they were assembled in the town hall, he made a speech. The goings-on at the grotto, he said, were absurd and a slap at the Bishop's authority as well as at his own. He stood at the crossroads. But he stood for His Majesty, the French Emperor, and his duty was plain. He wanted action. The local police would promptly clean out the grotto, and anyone claiming to have seen visions would be arrested and sent to the hospital at Tarbes for treatment as a mental case.

The Prefect looked around him. Had he made himself clear?

The thirty-seven mayors and other high officials nodded. Only the mayor of Lourdes and his police chief looked a little worried.

After the meeting the chief called the road mender and ordered him to get a horse and cart to remove the stuff from the grotto.

The schoolmistress, who happened to pass by, over-heard their talk and set out at once to rescue her "Madonna of the Birds" and her Sacred Heart image. She could tell hardly anyone in her hurry, but, when the road mender started making the round of cart-owners in town, doors slammed in his face just as fast as he could say what he wanted the cart for.

By the time he came to the blacksmith, he had learned his lesson. Without mentioning any purpose, he simply said the mayor would like to use the smith's horse and cart. The smith, glad to oblige the mayor, hitched up his old gray mare, and the road mender drove away.

The blacksmith had a daughter who loved the old horse. She was at home with her mother, unaware of all this, when she heard the neighbor children yell outside the window: "May the devil break your horse's neck!"

"Mother," the child cried, "the mare will break her neck!" They ran to hear what had happened, and then they, too, hurried out to Massabieille.

On the forest road they caught up with the road mender, who was squatting on the cart, vainly trying to coax the mare into a trot. "Stop", screeched the blacksmith's daughter. She raced ahead to grab the rein. It was all he could do to keep her from turning the horse around.

"If that's what it's for," her mother yelled at the road mender, "we'll have nothing to do with it!"

"You'll get me in trouble", the man shouted back. "I have orders—"

Other women came on the run from Lourdes, and up from Massabieille came the schoolmistress, her treasures under her arm. "He's there, the devil", she told them, angrily pointing over her shoulder, and went back to town.

The others went ahead. Atop the big rock they found the chief of police with the constable and the gamekeeper, waiting for the cart. The chief saw the women coming and drew himself up until he looked even more impressive than usual. "Ladies, I advise you to withdraw. I am under high orders", he said with all the dignity he could muster. But when the big road mender drove up, he beckoned impatiently: "Come on—get off—let's go!"

The road mender shook his head. "If I go, they'll take the horse away", he said. A glance at the women, and especially at the child who defiantly clung to the gray mare, convinced the chief that this fear was not unreasonable. So he posted the road mender as sentry atop the cliff, while he led the rest of his forces down to strip the grotto.

It was five in the afternoon. Only about a dozen people were on their knees at the cave. Some took no notice at all. One woman kept looking up and muttering, "Shame. Oh, shame."

"Let's go", said the chief. It annoyed him to see his constable kneel and sneak a drink from the spring, instead of doing his duty. "Let's get this over with", he said.

The gamekeeper followed the constable's example. They both dawdled so long that the chief decided to make a start himself. He walked up to the sanctuary lamp, extinguished it, and took it off the wire. Then he turned to one of the plaster statues of the Virgin, but he no sooner got his hands on it than it slipped and crashed in a thousand pieces. He was so stunned that his clay pipe fell from his mouth and broke, too.

After that, he touched nothing any more and merely repeated like a parrot, "Come on. Hurry up. Get it over with. Come on."

Reverently, the constable took down the flower-bedecked little Virgin in the shell. The gamekeeper took the third one. Neither broke a thing. They removed pictures, statues, countless rosaries and candles, two old church candlesticks, flowers, prayer books, silver chains, and a watch donated by a young woman who had since died. They put everything in boxes and carried them up to the cart. Most of the women had left, even the blacksmith's wife. But her daughter was still there, petting the old gray mare, and when they told her to go home, too, she just glared at them and stayed.

In the end, the grotto was bare—a chill, gloomy cave as of old. At the entrance, where the alms-box had been, there was now a large sign:

ALL DUMPING HERE IS FORBIDDEN.
OFFENDERS WILL BE PUNISHED.

On the road back to Lourdes, there were clusters of angry people. The chief walked ahead, looking neither right nor left. On the cart the road mender kept saying, "I just want to get the horse back." The game-keeper walked alongside the cart, and the constable secretly picked up a rosary and slid the beads through his fingers.

At the bridge, some thirty quarry workers stood rubbing their hands as the party came in sight. The blacksmith's girl was very scared, but she kept close to the horse. "Don't be scared", she whispered in the mare's ear. "They won't hurt us."

They didn't. Only after the cart had crossed the bridge, one shouted, "If we'd been there, you'd be looking for your horse and cart in the river."

When the iron gates of the town hall had closed behind the cart, the officials took off their caps and wiped the sweat off their faces. Outside, the black-smith's girl was waiting for her gray mare.

The Prefect's second order seemed even more ticklish to carry out. "Anyone claiming to have seen vi-sions—" there could be no doubt about the first and foremost one. And if clearing the grotto had so upset the people, how were they going to take Bernadette's arrest?

The unhappy officials decided to appeal to the parish priest. The mayor and the imperial prosecutor went to tell him what they had been ordered to do, for the good of religion as well as of peace and order.

The Curé shook his head. "The Prefect has no right to have the child arrested."

"Oh, we'd do nothing unlawful", said the prosecutor.

"You would do something unjust", the priest said, raising his voice.

The mayor said he did not like the idea, either, but if he did not obey a direct order from the Prefect, he would have to resign. Anyway, Bernadette would not be taken to jail—just to a hospital for treatment of her mind.

"I talked with the child several times", replied the priest. "She was always calm, clear, and consistent. Her mind is all right."

"But the doctors say she has hallucinations!" The prosecutor was not calm at all.

The Curé of Lourdes rose and looked down on the officials of the state. "Is it up to the doctors or to the Church to decide whether Bernadette has seen the Blessed Virgin?"

There was a moment of silence. The mayor looked stricken. "But we can't wait for the decision of the Church", he ventured at last. "The crowds are getting out of hand—"

"Without the use of force, I can answer for my parishioners", said Father Peyramale. "If you use force, I cannot."

"But—but what can we do?" the mayor stammered, wringing his hands.

And the prosecutor jumped up and hissed, "We *must* carry out the order!"

The priest raised his hands—in defense, not as a blessing. "This child is one of my flock", he said quietly, but his eyes seemed to burn through the two before him. "You may tell the Prefect that his men will find me at her door and will arrest her only over my dead body."

11

FAREWELL ACROSS THE RIVER

THE NEWS FROM LOURDES hurt the Prefect. So those stubborn peasants and their ungrateful parish priest wanted the little nuisance around? Well, they could have her. The authorities would merely maintain law and order. The police of Lourdes received new instructions: to leave Bernadette alone, but to make quite sure that no trace of the lawless chapel remained at the grotto. "I am on burning ground, but I walk without fear", said the Prefect.

Obediently, the police chief and the road mender returned to Massabieille. They found they had forgotten to remove the wooden railing that made the place look so much like an altar, but they also found they had forgotten to bring a hatchet. So the road mender borrowed one at the mill.

When the miller heard what had been done with his hatchet, it upset him so much that he dropped a plank on his foot. In no time, word was all over town that both his legs had been crushed. It went to show, people said, that anyone helping to violate the grotto would be punished. The blacksmith, though he denied it, was widely believed to have fallen into the hayloft and broken two ribs; some even said four ribs. To his gray mare, especially bad accidents were prophesied. They might have happened, too, if his daughter had not watched so well over the horse.

To calm the people, the town crier went through the streets to announce that the seized things could now be reclaimed by their owners. They all promptly showed up at the town hall and took along whatever they could get. The dead young woman's watch had vanished, but everything else was returned.

An hour later, half of it was back at the grotto.

Dutifully, the police cleaned out the place once more, under cover of a cloudburst. They got wetter than if the quarrymen had thrown them into the river, the constable grumbled. The only official who could see a silver lining was the mayor, who had at last persuaded the Prefect to let a chemist analyze the grotto water. Lourdes might yet become a health resort.

Bernadette, meanwhile, was going to a real health resort. It was the Curé's idea. Her cough worried him, and, besides, things might quiet down while she was away. Her parents could not pay for the trip, of course, but the Bishop agreed that it might be good for the parish. The Curé arranged for her to go to a small watering place high in the mountains, with her cousin Jeanne-Marie going along to watch.

The responsibility frightened Jeanne-Marie a little. "What will you do if the Lady tells you to go back to the grotto?" she asked her cousin as they left the Old Jail.

"I'll ask permission from Monsieur the Curé", Bernadette answered without hesitating.

A woman with a sick child came up to her. She was the neighbor who swept the streets of the town, and the child was the one the doctor had given two months to live, at the most. The time was just about up.

"He's getting worse every day", the mother lamented. "He won't live till you get back. Couldn't you bless him?"

"I'm no priest", Bernadette said.

"Touch him, at least", begged the woman.

Bernadette looked at the infant she had so often held in her arms and shook her head. "If you believe in God," she told the mother, "he'll be healed." Then she and Jeanne-Marie ran to the market place, to get on the stagecoach.

That night, the sick child's mother came home from work and found her husband showing the baby to an old crone who lived next door. Her other children were asleep. "Give me your little one's shirt," said the old woman, "so I can measure him for his burial dress. He's about dead."

The mother burst into tears. "I'll take him to the grotto", she sobbed.

"You're mad", said her husband. "He's dead, or almost, and he'll die on the way."

"Living or dead," said the mother, "I'll take him to the grotto." She took the child out of the cradle, wrapped him in her apron, and carried him into the street, praying all the way to Massabieille.

There were only a few women there, kneeling in prayer under the constable's watchful eye. The water of the spring gathered in the basin and ran out in three small streams. The street cleaner knelt down and prayed. Then she went to the basin. She made the Sign of the Cross, stripped the apron off the child, took the stiff little body in her two hands, and let the icy water run over it.

"Take that child out of the water!" a woman screamed.

"She wants to kill him", shrugged another. "That'll be one less; she has others."

The street cleaner stubbornly kept her child in the water. "I'll do what I can", she muttered. "The good God and the Blessed Virgin will help me."

The constable looked away, unable to interfere and unable to watch. The child did not move, although he went on breathing. At last the mother took him out, wrapped him in her apron again, and left. She said the rosary all the way home.

At home she called to her husband to warm a blanket for the baby. He took a glance and turned away. "Warm it yourself", he said in despair. "He's as nearly dead as when you left."

All through the night the mother kept watch by the cradle. At the first glimmer of dawn, she looked at the baby and thought she could see him smile. Before sunrise he drank a little.

She was making the beds when her husband called excitedly. For a moment, her heart tightened in mortal fear: was the child dead? Was he dying?

The cradle rocked gently. Before her eyes, the child climbed out and started crawling to her.

Bernadette's mother and some others were at the bake-house that morning, washing the linen of the baker's wife, when the street cleaner burst in with her kicking, wriggling baby. She wanted the doctor to see him, she happily cried. He was taking milk. He was moving around. He was cured!

The women all dropped their washing and ran out to spread the news.

The police chief heard it at breakfast, when the constable radiantly came to tell him that the doctor had confirmed another miracle. The chief jumped as though stung by a wasp. He almost upset the breakfast table. Had not even Bernadette admitted that the doctor's miracles were fairy tales?

"I'll lock him up for spreading false rumors", the chief bellowed as he buttoned up his uniform to go to Massabieille.

A shocking sight met his eyes. The crowd was as large as in the fortnight of the visions. The cave was again overflowing with pictures, candles, crosses, flowers, rosaries, and coins. "After all these days," the chief reported sadly, "this simple false rumor has been enough to put us back where we started!"

The Prefect threw the report into the wastebasket. Perhaps, he thought, the mayor was made of sterner stuff. He sent him orders to close the cave entirely: barricade the entrance, post a twenty-four-hour guard to arrest trespassers, and, in particular, let no one use the water. For, said the prudent Prefect, until one knew the result of the analysis the mayor had wisely requested, there really was no assurance that the water was not bad for people's health.

The mayor summoned his courage and a few carpenters and obeyed. He had the men put up a barrier and a stout pole with a sign: NO TRESPASSING. Then he left the constable as guard.

In front of the barrier, the constable walked up and down, up and down between the grotto and the people he was to keep out. Look the other way", they suggested. "Just for a minute."

"Go away", he said. "I'm on duty."

"You can't arrest all of us", they said, and this was certainly true.

So he took out his notebook. "I'll write down your names if you go in, and you'll be summoned before the judge."

He was as good as his word. Dutifully he put down the name of everybody he caught squeezing past the barrier. Only now and then he had to silence some woman at one end—and if just then a man with a bottle climbed over the other end, how could he see him? Not even policemen have eyes in the backs of their heads.

Eventually, he had a few quiet moments. He looked at the pole with the sign. Suddenly his eyes popped. What a coincidence, he thought.

It was the pole that had lain around the police station since Bernadette's father, falsely accused of stealing it, had spent his fortnight in jail.

The street cleaner came up the alley with her infant and stopped as though frozen to the ground. Before her stood Bernadette. "You're back!" gasped the woman. "No one told me—"

She had not seen anyone but her parents, Bernadette said. The Curé was giving a retreat to the children who were to make their First Communion, and she must not think of anything but that.

The street cleaner held up her squirming baby. "Did you know? He's cured! The spring cured him. But of course you know—you told me", she said, wide-eyed, and made a move as though to kneel before the little girl.

"Don't!" said Bernadette sharply. "Thank our Lady. I didn't know. I'm so glad. Aren't you? What's wrong?"

The woman was weeping bitterly. She had been to the grotto again, she sobbed. They had taken her name, and now she would be called before the judge and sent to jail.

"Don't worry, they'll let you go", Bernadette said and went home to study her catechism. She still could not read it properly. She still feared her ignorance might bar her from Holy Communion, and she promised the chaplain to study even harder afterward. But, in fact, the Curé—who sent at least as many reports to Tarbes, in those days, as the police chief— seemed more favorably impressed the more he saw of her. "Her development makes astonishing strides", he informed the Bishop.

The long-awaited day of her First Communion came on another Thursday. It was the Feast of Corpus Christi, and the procession moved through the streets of Lourdes with the little statue of the Virgin that Pauline's family had brought back from the grotto when it had been boarded up. And when the day was over, the parish priest wrote to Tarbes: "Bernadette seemed wholeheartedly conscious of the solemnity and significance of the occasion."

To his chaplain, however, he said, "I wonder, I wonder. She talked—she believes she talked with the Holy Mother of God. Can she help thinking less of the Blessed Sacrament she has now received from the Church?"

"I'll ask her", said the little chaplain.

"I wonder whether you should", Father Peyramale said with a worried frown. "You know if she prefers the vision, it proves her unworthy to receive the Body and Blood of Christ in the Holy Eucharist. But if she prefers the sacrament, the vision cannot have been our Lady."

The chaplain nodded. "I'll ask her", he said again.

And, after Bernadette's next confession, he did ask her. "Which made you happier: to receive Holy Communion or to talk with the Blessed Virgin?"

"I don't know", the child said simply. "Things like that go together and can't be compared. All I know is that I was very happy both times."

"Thank you, my child", said the confessor.

"Take Mouton along", the police chief advised the constable. "He'll help you deal with the crowd."

Mouton was the constable's dog. He was not handsome, but he was greatly respected by those who had reason to fear the law. Indeed, when the two were on official business, it often looked as if Mouton were the policeman and the constable his aide. So Mouton went on grotto duty.

It had a strange effect on him. He never growled at anyone out there. He wagged his tail when people sneaked into the cave. And, on the way to Massabieille, he would leave his master at the bridge and race ahead, where he was received with joy—especially by the children, who had always been a little afraid of Mouton. "The Blessed Virgin must want him to play that trick", panted the constable, as he ran after his dog.

The children were getting out of hand. Those who should have been in school knelt along the river banks with candles or went in procession through town and countryside, twisting their faces and shrieking about their visions. They claimed to see devils, oddly dressed Virgins, and whole Holy Families. One night a group paraded down to the grotto and yelled at the people there: "All of you say your rosaries! The good God will recite it!"

The constable stopped that nonsense. "The good God say the rosary? Is the world upside down? Scat, you creatures of Satan", he shouted, and Mouton barked so fiercely that the procession fled before any of the grown-ups were taken in.

The mayor was fuming. The Prefect held him responsible for keeping the grotto closed—and the grotto would not stay closed. Every few days now, when the guard on duty went to lunch or dinner, the barrier would be torn down and the pieces thrown into the river. Besides, the mayor's dream of a health resort had just been shattered by the chemist's report: the spring, it said, produced good drinking water, with nothing in it that could explain any cures. In desperation, the mayor turned on the children. He could handle those, at least. He gave orders to stop their pranks by all means, to arrest every child in Lourdes, if necessary, and not to worry about overcrowding the jail. The parents would get them out all right, he assured the police.

It was a good plan, but things happened too quickly. Before any local child could be arrested, others came across the mountains, from places where the mayor had nothing to say. A boy of ten led processions to Massabieille—on a mission, he said, to bring the Blessed Virgin from Lourdes into his valley. The crusade reached a peak on the fourth of July, which was the local feast of Lourdes. The townspeople had just gone down to celebrate, to smash the barrier once more and uproot the pole with the sign, when the boy came with his followers. He went into the grotto, and a moment later not only he but everyone around heard a somewhat squeaky voice that said, "My child, in your valley there are many good people; at Lourdes there is nothing but rabble."

Of course, this did not please the people of Lourdes. Litanies were halted by arguments; children raced around, howling; the police made arrests; and the mayor wrung his hands at this new disaster. He went to the judge and asked for the immediate trial of all those charged with trespassing at the grotto, spreading false rumors, and related crimes. There were nearly eighty of them, and the mayor hoped that such wholesale justice might throw a scare into others.

Almost all the accused were women, among them the Soubirous' neighbors: the baker's wife, the cobbler's wife, and the street cleaner. All were badly frightened. The trial was held on a bright summer day in a courtroom packed with defendants and spectators and gendarmes. The women hid their faces in their shawls, sobbing as the black-robed prosecutor read the charges. They sounded terrible, especially in French, which not all of them understood. When a woman kept interrupting in patois, her own lawyer snarled at the others, "Keep that accursed hag quiet!"

In a rear row, her baby in her arms, sat the street cleaner. When the judge started questioning the women, one by one, she trembled. But then she remembered that Bernadette had told her not to worry, and when she heard the men in the black robes snap at some poor woman whose voice failed her with fright, she became angrier and angrier.

Finally her name was called. "You went to the grotto like the rest?"

She said, "I don't know about the rest, Your Honor, but I'd like to tell you what I think about it—"

"Don't talk so much, or I'll send you to jail", said the judge.

The woman straightened up. "All right, Your Honor. I don't eat bread every day; in jail I'll have it, and meat once a week. You called me—"

"I know enough. You went to the grotto."

"You called me—let me have my say!" She held up the smiling baby, so the whole courtroom could see it. "My child here was dying. They told me to bury him. But I bathed him in the grotto water—and look at him now!"

The judge glanced up and shrugged. "As you bathed the child in this water, I'll have to deal with you according to law", he said and searched his papers for the next case. It had gradually become quite dark.

"Deal with me any way you like, Your Honor", said the woman. "We went only on common land that belongs to you and me. It's not so long since the rich man's hog and the poor man's sow both went to Massabieille. We're all equal there." She looked at her child again. "And he was dead, and he's cured!"

The judge fumbled with his papers. There was a violent thunderclap. He looked up, dumbfounded. Then he rose from the bench, mumbled, "Acquitted. All are acquitted", and walked out.

The women sat stunned, until people around started clapping and some said that the Blessed Virgin had protected them. But the baker's wife chuckled to her friends: "These gentlemen are not so different from us! They're afraid of the thunder."

When they emerged on the street, the storm had passed. The sky was as clear as before. The women chattered a while, and then they scattered. The three neighbors walked home together. In the alley they met Bernadette, who laughed and called to the street cleaner, "I told you they'd let you go!"

And the word went around town and all over the province. "Those sorceresses of Lourdes have won their case", people said to each other, in anger, with glee, or with pride.

On the following day—it was a Friday and the Feast of Our Lady of Mount Carmel—four children roaming the woods near Massabieille came upon a procession that followed a little girl. The four were Bernadette's playmates who had been with her at the second vision: Catherine, the pretty one; Marie, who had carried the holy water; Pauline, who had run away; and Jeanne, who had dropped the rock.

Atop the cliff, the girl commanded her followers to kiss the ground. They were just getting up again when the four playmates came in sight. "There's someone here who hasn't kissed the ground", cried the little girl.

Flustered, Catherine dropped to her knees. So did Marie and Pauline. Then Jeanne came around the bend.

"Halt!" cried the girl. "Withdraw! The Blessed Virgin doesn't want you to come nearer."

Jeanne turned white. "The rock", she moaned. "She won't ever forgive me—" And she staggered back into the woods.

Pauline ran after her. On the forest road she caught up and gripped Jeanne's sob-racked shoulders. "That's foolishness", she said earnestly. "Don't you believe it. It can't be true."

Slowly they walked back to Lourdes. "It is true", Jeanne sighed. "It's where I dropped the rock. Now the Blessed Virgin doesn't want me around."

Pauline shook her head. "That can't be true", she said again, firmly. "The Blessed Virgin loves us all."

In the late afternoon of the same Friday, July 16, Bernadette prayed in the parish church. Through her fingers ran the poor rosary Our Lady had once preferred, long ago. For fourteen weeks and two days she had not seen the vision and had not been to the grotto that was now boarded up completely with strong lumber, all the way to the top. Now, suddenly, the beads in her hand began to tremble. The Lady was calling!

The mountains cast long shadows over the valley as Bernadette left the church. She went to the inn for Aunt Bernarde's blessed candle, and the godmother came right along; in the street the postmaster's girls, Rosine and Dominiquette, saw them and followed.

Swiftly the four slipped out of town, past the Citadel and down the hill to the river. They headed not for the bridge but for the meadows on the right bank, across the swirling water from the barricaded cave of Massabieille. A group of women knelt in the dusk, praying in silence.

The candlelight flickered faintly on Bernadette's face. Her joined hands fell in a startled little move: there! there was the golden glow, the pair of golden roses, the white veil flowing in the wind, the blue sash shining in the dark—there was Our Lady of the Grotto . . . Bernadette had never seen her so lovely. She did not speak; she only smiled. She raised her hands to heaven and bade farewell to the child who knelt below.

Once again Bernadette smiled through the tears that ran down her face. She got up slowly. It was dark in the valley.

"How could you see her?" Rosine asked. "The river is so wide, and the barrier so high!"

"I saw neither the river nor the barrier", Bernadette said. "I saw only the Blessed Virgin."

12

THE OTHER WORLD

F OUR DAYS LATER Bernadette was called to the parish house. A bishop from another part of France was passing through and wished to see her. She went at once, poorly dressed as ever in plain cotton, with a cotton apron, a large cotton kerchief around her neck and another on her head, knotted under the chin, and *sabots* and woolen stockings on her feet.

The Bishop of Montpellier awaited her in Father Peyramale's study. The Curé and the chaplain were there, too. She greeted them all with the same respect, but the chaplain and even the Curé seemed unusually tongue-tied in the presence of the guest in the purple robes.

He glanced sympathetically at the little girl. "So, you are the child who has seen the Blessed Virgin?"

"Yes", Bernadette said. It sounded natural, happy, and modest.

He asked for the story, and she told it in her usual brief fashion—"out of any three words, Bernadette usually keeps back two", people said in Lourdes. The chaplain sat with his hands folded and his eyes cast down; the Curé kept his on the Bishop. The Bishop listened silently until Bernadette closed her story with the final farewell.

"And you won't see the Lady of the grotto again?" he asked after a brief pause.

She shook her head and looked upward with longing. "Never."

The Bishop cleared his throat. "The police and the others were very hard on you", he said.

Bernadette looked down again. "I don't remember that."

"Show me your rosary", he said. She drew the shabby beads from her pocket. "How did the Vision hold hers?" he wanted to know.

Bernadette seemed to change before his eyes. She

straightened up, clasped her hands, and moved the beads between her right thumb and forefinger. Her lips were closed, like the Lady's, but a smile of bliss hovered about them. It was no longer a poor, sickly child who stood before the Bishop of Montpellier.

He asked, "Did she change her position when she was not saying the rosary?"

Bernadette opened her arms, let them sink down her sides, and turned the palms outward.

The Bishop was startled. He reached for a gold medal he was wearing. "So, the Vision stood just as our Lady is shown here?" he asked. He handed the medal to the child.

Bernadette looked attentively at the little image. "Yes", she said. Then, pointing at the radiating lines on the medal, she added, "But she had nothing like that on her hands."

The Bishop took back his medal and offered her a rosary. It was a thing of beauty, with rose-colored corals strung on a chain of gold. His Holiness the Pope himself had blessed it, he said. The chaplain's eyes bulged; he had never seen so beautiful a rosary. The Curé's eyes were on Bernadette.

"It's yours", the Bishop graciously urged her. "I'm grateful to you for your account of the visions. Take the rosary."

The child bowed deeply. "Thank you, my lord, but I have one."

The little chaplain was stunned. The Curé smiled.

The Bishop rose and touched Bernadette's forehead, making her look up again. The dark, shabby old rosary remained in her hand.

"Did the Blessed Virgin talk to you about heaven?" asked the prince of the Church.

"She said I wouldn't be happy in this world, but in another", Bernadette answered simply.

"Well," said the Bishop, "if she promised you happiness in the other world, what do you have to worry about in this one? You just rely on that promise."

It sounded like a statement, not like a question, but Bernadette's eyes widened in astonishment. "Oh, no, my lord", she said quickly. "Now I have to deserve it!"

And the Bishop raised his precious rosary once more, to bless the child.

When she left, he looked after her for a time without speaking. The two priests of Lourdes waited quietly. At last, his eyes still on the door through which Bernadette had gone out, the Bishop murmured to himself: "The last shall be first . . ."

Then he turned to the parish priest. "Your superiors still refuse to investigate this?"

Father Peyramale nodded.

"I had not intended to stop at Tarbes," said the Bishop, "but now my conscience forces me to do so. It's a matter of duty. I'll go and see your Bishop, and if any doubts linger in his mind, I'll tell him to come to Lourdes. There must have been reasons for his silence and reserve, but from now on they're out of place. At all costs the diocesan authority must speak out."

The Curé of Lourdes thanked the Bishop of Montpellier. His little chaplain thanked God.

A week passed. Then, early one afternoon, company came to the Old Jail. A distinguished looking woman with a nun and three small girls wanted to see Bernadette. The lady and the children were so well-dressed that Louise Soubirous, who took the party upstairs, kept mumbling apologies for the dark hallway and the wobbly steps.

Bernadette curtsied twice—first to the good sister, then to the noble lady. The lady asked graciously about her family and her daily life before she mentioned the grotto. She was going to take her children there now. Would Bernadette come along?

Bernadette shook her head. "I've been forbidden."

Because they were strangers, however, she agreed to show them to the bridge. The gaping neighbors saw her walk down the alley arm in arm with the great lady. But at the bridge Bernadette said good-bye and stood looking after the group that disappeared toward Massabieille.

Neither a nun's habit nor the most elegant Parisian gown could make the constable forget his duty. He waited until the strangers had finished praying before the boarded-up grotto; then he went and asked for their names. The sister gave that of her convent. The lady said she was an admiral's widow and the governess of His Imperial Highness, the little crown prince. They had just come from the Emperor's summer palace on the Bay of Biscay.

The constable's hand flew to his cap in a salute before he jotted down the illustrious names.

The admiral's widow produced a crystal bottle. "May I have some water from the spring now?" she asked as if it were the most natural thing in the world.

"But, Madame," stammered the constable, "my orders—they're from the Prefect himself—"

The lady looked at him as a governess would look at a silly little boy. "The water is for Her Majesty, the Empress, herself", she said pointedly.

The constable's knees shook. He saluted again, took the bottle, knelt down where the spring ran out under the barrier, and returned the full bottle with another salute. The lady gave him a tip and left with the nun and the children.

The constable mopped his brow.

So did the chief of police, when he heard that he should take an Imperial governess into court for drawing water for the Empress. His predicament was bad enough as it was. Only this morning he had learned that the Bishop of Tarbes, in the Holy Name of God, would appoint a commission to investigate the happenings at the grotto. What, in the name of all the saints, was the chief to do? He could seek instructions from the Prefect. But how could he even ask such impossible questions as whether he should arrest the Bishop's commission? And the governess of the prince? It took him hours to find a diplomatic wording: "Should an exception be made, or should the general law be applied to them, too?"

The Prefect was the third to mop his brow, when he received this inquiry. For several days he was at a loss what to say. To his relief, the same days brought a falling off in the reports of visions and similar nuisances from the Lourdes district. So the Prefect decided that an official's duty in these difficult circumstances was to refrain from personal judgment and to wait till Providence revealed the truth.

At Lourdes, meanwhile, new types of pilgrims were seen. Many priests came, now that the Bishop's action had opened the door, and many prominent laymen. The chaplain would show them the road to Massabieille, always careful to stop at the bridge, as Bernadette had done, and to point out that the cave was closed by the authorities. Some went, anyway, but most of them were more curious about the child. They came to see or to argue, to listen or to ask questions, to pray or to scoff.

"Look here," a priest from a nearby town said to her, "I don't believe you saw the Blessed Virgin."

Bernadette remained silent.

"Well, have you nothing to say?"

"What do you want me to say, Father?"

"You should make me believe that you saw her."

"She told me to tell people what I saw", Bernadette said. "She didn't tell me to make them believe it."

Her words convinced the priest.

She kept her promise to the chaplain and went on studying faithfully after her First Communion, but her progress remained slow. A gentleman of Lourdes undertook to teach her French but threw up his hands when she could not even keep the letters in mind. "It would be less trouble driving the book through your head than getting you to remember your lesson", he told her in despair.

The Curé felt that the Old Jail was no place for Bernadette any more. With all these visitors, it might reflect poorly on his parish. He arranged for a vacant mill to be rented to her father, who had once been a miller by trade; it was the worst mill in town, but, after the Old Jail, it seemed like a palace. At last François Soubirous could support his family again. And Bernadette had a little room of her own now, poorly furnished, but brightened by the flowers of a small shrine, with our Lady's statue in the center.

In September, on the Feast of Our Lady's Nativity, the girl with the worst background in town became a member of the Children of Mary. Her sponsors were Mademoiselle Estrade, the late chairlady's friend, and the widow who had thought the chairlady was haunting Massabieille. And the seamstress took care of her proper white dress, veil, and blue ribbon.

On October 5, at three in the afternoon, the town

crier and the drummer marched through the town in dress uniform and gloves. At every corner the drummer beat a brief roll, and the crier read: "By order of the Emperor . . ."

People hung out of windows and rushed out of doors to listen.

"People of Lourdes! You were impatiently awaiting the day when the grotto would be reopened. That day has come", shouted the crier. "From now on you may freely enter the grotto!"

Cheers echoed through the town. People hugged and kissed each other. They took bottles and pitchers and jars and headed for the grotto. The road mender came with a cart, and when he said it was to remove the barrier, the blacksmith rushed out with his old gray mare and insisted that she have the honor. His daughter ran ahead of a delirious crowd of children. By nightfall every man, woman, and child in Lourdes had prayed and drunk at the spring. They kissed the ground and lifted up their faces to the cave—and there was Bernadette, kneeling and bathing her eyes in the water. "What do you do that for?" the people asked, astonished.

She looked up, smiling. "To make me learn to read", she said, putting some more water on her eyes.

And some, with powerful voices, recited the rosary, and the kneeling crowd responded, on and on into the night.

From that day on, to the happy surprise of the

officials, there were no more visions, children's processions, or other disturbances anywhere around Lourdes.

In mid-November, Bernadette was called to Massabieille by the eight priests who made up the Bishop's commission. They sent for her in secret, but half the town was there by the time she arrived. People were kneeling all around the grotto and the rock while Bernadette once more patiently answered questions.

"You must be very proud of having seen the Blessed Virgin", said one of the eight.

"Why? She just took me for a servant", the girl replied.

"Indeed? What wages does she pay you?"

"Oh," Bernadette said, "we haven't made the contract yet."

"Well, what do you think she'll give you after she's tried you out?"

"I think she won't be satisfied", the girl said. "She'll dismiss me."

The questioner was satisfied. But another priest wanted to know why would the Virgin have picked her, of all people, for a servant?

Bernadette lowered her head. "If our Lady could have found a greater fool than I, she would have chosen her."

The Bishop's commission had not yet finished its work when the Curé decided that life at home was too strenuous for Bernadette. She was now sixteen;

he thought she would be better off as a boarder at the hospice. One who disagreed was the doctor. He knew that the Mother Superior had disliked the girl ever since her catechism class. "Bernadette is being put in bad hands", lamented the doctor.

With the sisters, Bernadette no longer led a child's life. She helped in the kitchen and in the hospital, and whatever she might be doing was continually interrupted by curious visitors. By then, she had learned not only to read and write but to speak French; she could answer without having someone to interpret for her, but the constant interviews left her more and more exhausted. The pains in her chest grew worse. She started spitting blood. "Open my chest and let me breathe", she cried when the attacks became too bad.

But she never lost her temper or her patience, and she never refused an interview the sisters asked of her. One day, as one of them led her to the parlor again, she leaned her head against the closed door and wept. "I'm just a curiosity—!"

"Courage", said the nun. "Those are very big tears." And Bernadette dried them and walked in, smiling, for her interview.

At eighteen, she was so sick that she was given the Last Sacraments. "Don't you want to try the water of the spring?" a young nun asked her.

She shook her head with an effort. "It's not for me—"

"Why not?" the sister wanted to know.

"Our Lady wants me to suffer", Bernadette said, when she could breathe again. But, as the attack passed, she lay back and sighed, "It's as if a mountain were lifted off my chest."

Soon after this, the Bishop of Tarbes rendered his judgment on her visions. "We declare", he said in a pastoral letter, "that Mary, the Immaculate Mother of God, truly appeared to Bernadette Soubirous on February 11, 1858, and on subsequent days in the grotto of Massabieille near the town of Lourdes; that these appearances have all the character of truth; and that the faithful are justified in believing them certain."

The Bishop's letter went to all the bishops of France, with an appeal for their support and aid in the work of building a chapel on the spot of the visions. A famous sculptor was hired to make a statue of Bernadette's Lady for the niche where the child had seen her. He had great confidence in his art and thought he could model a statue that would make the girl cry out, "It's she!" Bernadette did her best to mirror the Lady for him, as she had done for the Bishop of Montpellier, but she could not make the sculptor see as the Bishop had seen. When they showed her the finished statue, she said, "It's not at all like Our Lady of the Grotto."

Even so, she looked forward eagerly to its unveiling, when a solemn procession was to move out to the grotto. Before the great day, however, the Curé said she was not well enough and forbade her to take part. "I must be harsh", he explained to the chaplain. "The crowds would hail her too much. I must preserve her from pride."

At the day's end, Cousin Jeanne-Marie came to tell Bernadette all about the celebration. The bells had tolled from every steeple in the valley, and sixty thousand persons had marched from the parish church to Massabieille, through the garlanded, flag-bedecked, flower-strewn streets of Lourdes. Only two had been missing: the Curé, suddenly taken ill, too, and poor Bernadette.

The sick girl had heard the bells; now she listened happily to the description. "I was at the grotto with you in spirit", she said. "Don't feel sorry for me. When one is doing God's will, one doesn't complain."

She did not look so terribly ill that she couldn't have gone, observed her cousin. Who had forbidden it—the doctor?

"It was Monsieur the Curé," Bernadette said, "but the Blessed Virgin has got him well in hand. She's sent him a nice stomachache to keep him in bed."

Once again, they were just two girlfriends talking.

Bernadette helped in the kitchen, in the hospital, and all around the hospice. Once, she was sent from the kitchen to answer the doorbell, and a bishop stood outside. She bowed so humbly that he said, *"Prou,*

prou, prou"—which was patois for "That'll do!"—and the girl burst out laughing to hear a strange bishop speak the patois of her valley. Then the Mother Superior came and sent her straight back to the kitchen, where she still had a mountain of carrots to grate.

Minutes later, she was amazed to see the Bishop ushered into the kitchen. Bernadette sat on a block of wood in the chimney corner, bent over her carrots. The Mother Superior called her, introduced her by name, and mentioned casually that the illustrious guest was the Bishop of Nevers, the superior of the sisters of the hospice. He smiled kindly at the frail, poorly dressed girl. The Mother Superior did not smile.

"My lord," she said, "allow me to complete your information by telling you what the Blessed Virgin has not yet done for Bernadette—and that is convert her in earnest. Would you believe it: just now the young lady and I had quite a talk. She wanted to throw the peelings into this bucket rather than that one. Well, I almost thought I'd have to give in to her!"

Tears welled up in Bernadette's eyes. "Dear Mother," she said, "once more I beg your pardon."

The Mother Superior ignored her. "With all the free graces she has received, poor Bernadette is preparing herself for purgatory. You'd be doing a work of charity in praying for her improvement", she told the Bishop and left him alone with the girl.

"Now, my child," he began, "what are you going to become?"

She was greatly astonished. "Why, nothing, my lord."

"Nothing? But one must do something in this world."

"Well," she said, "I'm here with the sisters."

"Don't you think of going out into the world again?" he asked. "A suitable marriage, perhaps?"

"Oh, no, no", she cried. "Not that!"

"Or would you like to enter a convent?"

She hung her head. "I've no money. I wouldn't be able to bring a dowry to the convent."

"You can make up for that in other ways", said the Bishop.

Bernadette blushed deeply. "But I know nothing. I'm good at nothing."

"Come, come", said the Bishop. "I just saw you grating carrots."

When she remained silent, he told her to think it over and pray. If her heart said yes, she should ask the Mother Superior to notify him; he would take care of the rest. Bernadette thought it over and prayed. She felt a longing for the religious life, but she was a little afraid of the strict Sisters of Nevers. She was unable to reach a decision until Jeanne-Marie, by then a village school teacher in the vicinity, came to visit with great news for her cousin: she had made up her mind to enter religion!

Bernadette embraced her. Even before blurting out her own problem, she knew that her heart had spoken. They talked earnestly about the various Orders. Jeanne-Marie was still wavering between the Trappistines and Discalced Carmelites; Bernadette only hoped that whichever Order her cousin chose would accept her.

When Bernadette applied for admission to the Carmelite nuns, however, she was turned down. Her health was not considered strong enough. Eventually, she asked the Mother Superior to write to the Bishop of Nevers. True to his promise, he took it up with the Mother General of the Sisters of Nevers, but this nun, too, hesitated. "She hasn't the health", she said. "She would be in the hospital all the time. And then she can't do very much."

The Bishop smiled, a little absently. "She could always grate your carrots. I saw her doing that at Lourdes."

But when the Sisters of Nevers were ready at last to accept her, Bernadette was really too ill to make the long trip from her mountains to the plains of central France. She was ill for two years.

Bernadette was still in the hospice of Lourdes on Whit-Monday of 1866, when the chapel of Our Lady of the Grotto was to be consecrated. It was a beautiful morning. Pilgrims swarmed on every road around Lourdes; every house in town was decked out in wreaths and banners; triumphal arches had risen in the streets, along the route of the procession. Three

hundred priests started from the parish church for Massabieille, and when the Bishop of Tarbes and Father Peyramale appeared on top of the rock, the crowds burst into rousing cheers: "Long live the Bishop! Long live the Curé!"

This time Bernadette was allowed to take part in the celebration. She walked in the tightly grouped flock of the Children of Mary, like all of them in a white, blue-ribboned dress, her face half-hidden by a veil. She was all but invisible among them. At twenty-two, she was still the smallest of all.

Unnoticed, she got as far as the entrance of the new crypt. There the little chaplain saw her. "Look," he whispered to the Curé, "she is the same child she was at the time of the visions. Time has not touched her. She herself is a vision."

The Curé looked at Bernadette. A thousand eyes followed his. People dropped on their knees. A murmur ran through the crowd, swelling, rising: "The saint . . . our saint . . ."

Shocked, Bernadette hid her face in her hands. She fell down and kissed the ground, the beloved earth of Massabieille that she would so soon leave forever. Her eyes rose to the chapel of Our Lady of the Grotto. Would she never see her again?

Deep down in her heart she heard the voice: "Not in this world . . . but in another. . . ."

* * *

Today you can see them both—forever together. You can see Bernadette kneel adoringly before the niche, beneath the small bare feet with the golden roses, half-hidden under the white gown with the blue sash. Her left hand holds the blessed candle, her right the dark rosary. Eternally young and radiant, the Lady looks at the slum child she chose. Her eyes are blue.

"It isn't a work of art", says the old priest. "Just a faithful reproduction in plaster. It shows even the miraculous spring that has cured so many in Lourdes."

He points to a tiny basin. One hardly notices it in the twilight that fills the little church of Our Lady of Lourdes.

"Our chapel", the priest continues, "was built long before nineteen thirty-three, when Bernadette was canonized on the Feast of the Immaculate Conception. Now we celebrate Saint Bernadette's Day each year on the anniversary of her death, as with all saints. She departed this life on April sixteen, eighteen seventy-six, as suffering Sister Marie-Bernard of Nevers."

Distantly, as though all the way from France, one hears the roll of the surf along the beach where the Pilgrim Fathers first touched American soil. The sea around Cape Cod accompanies the old priest's story; he, too, came from the Old World.

"And now," he ends with a smile, "our Lady is the patroness of America under the title she chose as she revealed herself to the poorest child in France."

His hand moves in the dusk. Bernadette's candle lights up, and at the same time the halo around her Lady's head glows in the words she spoke to her little servant:

"I am the Immaculate Conception."